MOXIE

PHYLLIS ROSSITER

MOXIE

FOUR WINDS PRESS

New York

COLLIER MACMILLAN CANADA
Toronto

MAXWELL MACMILLAN INTERNATIONAL PUBLISHING GROUP
New York   Oxford   Singapore   Sydney

Four Winds Press
Macmillan Publishing Company
866 Third Avenue, New York, NY 10022
Collier Macmillan Canada, Inc.
1200 Eglinton Avenue East
Suite 200
Don Mills, Ontario M3C 3N1
First Edition
Printed in the United States of America

10 9 8 7 6 5 4 3 2 1

The text of this book is set in 12 point Century Old Style.

Library of Congress Cataloging-in-Publication Data
Rossiter, Phyllis.
Moxie / by Phyllis Rossiter. — 1st ed.   p.   cm.
Summary: Thirteen-year-old Drew, determined to help his family
hold on to their farm in the drought-stricken Dust Bowl of 1934,
stubbornly tends his livestock and refuses to give up hope.
ISBN 0-02-777831-2
[1. Droughts—Great Plains—Fiction.   2. Depressions—1929—Fiction.
3. Farm life—Kansas—Fiction.   4. Family problems—Fiction.]   I. Title.
PZ7.R7224Mo   1990   [Fic]—dc20 90-30027 CIP AC

To Dennis,

Whose own moxie got him through it the first time,
his love for me, the second.

CHAPTER **1**

"Turning thirteen on Friday the thirteenth is very bad luck!"

Drew Ralston let his armload of wood clatter into the box behind the cookstove. The racket drowned his sigh. "Mom, I was born on the thirteenth, so it must be my lucky number."

His mother sniffed. "Shoot. More likely it means you'll always be unlucky." She shoved a piece of wood into the stove and, using the tail of her apron to protect her hand from the heat, clanged the round iron lid back into place. Then she flipped her nighttime braid over her shoulder and turned to him, hands on hips.

Her high cheekbones and glossy black hair reminded Drew of an Indian princess—a very short one. "Well, anyway. Happy birthday, baby." She caught him in a hug and seemed about to kiss him.

He returned her hug briefly in honor of his birthday, then twisted out of her grasp. "I gotta get to school." He snatched his syrup-can lunch pail off the worktable and escaped. "Bye, Mom." He allowed the screen door to slam behind him.

On his lookout knoll a safe distance from the house, Drew stopped to admire the farm. No wonder Granddad chose this spot for his dugout, he thought.

The early sun rays spotlighted Drew and cast his shadow across the barnyard. A breeze too warm for April ruffled the curls around the edge of his cap. He wished he could hug this birthday morning and put it into an overall pocket to enjoy forever. He had longed to be thirteen, as though it had some of Mom's magic to make him taller, stronger, smarter. But nothing had changed. He was still too short to harness the horses, and Mom was still convinced he was doomed.

Poor Mom. Nobody else believed in all her charms and superstitions. She even thought that mirror she broke way back in 1930 had caused the depression. She had said, "Seven years of bad luck for breaking a mirror."

"Boy, if she's right that means three more years of depression," Drew said aloud. He sighed and knew he should go meet Jay. Dad would not like it if he was late for school again.

He scanned the vast horizon and circled the knoll for one last look at their land, flat as a table except toward the river where a few low hills pushed up like wrinkles elbowed into a tablecloth. Though he might wish to be taller or older or better looking, he never wanted to be anything but a farmer.

But if it did not rain soon, there would be no farm, he thought. Nor even any grass for pasture.

Drew kicked the knoll, and a dust devil sprang from his toe and danced away on the wind. Not even winter had broken the drought. This would be the second summer that the wheat field had yielded only dust. No wheat, no money.

And no new feed for the sheep. Could he fatten his lambs on the little feed they had left? For that matter, could he even keep the sheep healthy?

Drew shook his head. He should not waste such a frisky morning thinking black thoughts. He wanted to kick up his heels like one of his lambs.

The wail of the train to Wichita reminded him of the time, and he loped off the knoll. Once across the barnyard, he broad-jumped the pasture fence and crunched through the remains of last year's sun-dried grass.

Jay was not waiting on the path to school.

Drew dropped down on his favorite rock, already summer warm, to wait. The blue of the sky almost hurt his eyes. It seemed alive, to move and beckon to him.

The freight rumbled by; the ground trembled under its power. He had read that the Indians had called the steam engine "Iron Horse," but to him it looked more like a monstrous black buffalo. The stack fogged the sky with coal smoke, a black stain that trailed the length of the train and lingered to mark its track.

Drew stood on the rock to exchange waves with the engineer.

"It's my birthday!" he shouted.

A dog barked in the woods, and Jay burst out of the trees. His blue eyes seemed very large behind his thick glasses. The barking grew more and more excited.

"There's a snake yonder in the path," Jay said in a breathless voice that was surprisingly high and girlish—a fault he was painfully aware of. Drew had tried to tell him it sounded better than his own scratchy voice, which cracked at all the wrong times and humiliated him when he most wanted to seem grown up. Besides, at least Jay stood respectably tall, big boned and solid.

Drew followed Jay into the woods, where a big, black rat snake stretched across the path. Jay's dog, Billy Boy, barked at it without seeming to breathe.

Drew and Jay prodded the snake with sticks and bombed it with rocks, but it refused to budge.

"It's dead," Drew decided.

"Well, what's it doing here?" Jay's glasses slid down his nose, and he pushed them up and squinted at Drew.

"Dunno . . . I bet somebody put him here thinking to scare us."

"But who?" asked Jay.

"Hmm. Probably that Gordie Madsen." Drew had an inspiration. "Let's take him to school and scare the others."

Jay nudged the snake with a holey tennis shoe. "Sure he's dead?"

"Yeah, sure." Drew took hold of a length of snake in each hand. He worked to keep from tripping over the trailing end as he led the way along the path.

Jay hooked the bails of both lunch pails over one hand to leave the other hand free for pushing up his glasses and brushing the cornsilk hair out of his eyes. Billy Boy trotted behind, still growling a warning with every swing of the snake's head.

"Go home, Billy. Go on—get!" Jay shouted, and flailed his free arm every few steps until at last the dog obeyed.

Later Drew could not say whose idea it was, but by the time they cleared the woods and crossed the dusty road to the schoolhouse, they had a plan.

Behind the one-room building, the path forked. Each branch led to a twin backhouse. Teacher's hand-lettered sign on one door said Girls, and on the other, Boys.

While Jay kept watch, Drew coiled the snake on the floor of the girls' privy and propped its head on the topmost coil. From the doorway it looked menacingly alive.

Drew grinned. "That ought to scare the pants off the first girl coming down the path."

Jay giggled and scanned the prairie, empty to the horizon, for witnesses. Only an aged elm stood between them and the faded school building. "Nobody here yet; we must be early."

Absorbed in their snaky errand, they had dawdled less than usual along the way. Drew wiped his hands on his striped overalls and squatted on the ground under the sheltering tree. Jay, as always, shadowed him.

Drew gazed up into the few green leaves that had ventured into the hot wind. "Jay, spring has sprung. Sure hate to go to school on a day like this."

"Yeah. Wish it was a holiday."

"Well, it's my birthday. It ought to be a holiday." Drew's voice broke; he cleared his throat. "Do you suppose we'd have to go in if the bell didn't ring?" He could not remember a time when the bell had not rung except on holidays and weekends—and in the summer.

"But how you gonna keep the bell from ringing?" Jay wanted to know.

"I got me an idea." Drew could just see the belfry through the leaves.

Jay followed Drew's gaze. "How you gonna get up there?"

Drew had already reached into the tree towering above them, and Jay scrambled after him. A broken fingernail and two scraped elbows later, Drew stood puffing on the roof of the empty schoolhouse.

"How we gonna get down?" Jay asked, leaning out to check the distance to the ground.

"Worry about that later." Drew stretched over the belfry railing and gingerly took hold of the bell rope. It would not do for the bell to ring accidentally. Working slowly, he tied a big knot in the rope and then another one right over the first. "Bet she don't ring now." He grinned at Jay.

"*Now* how we gonna get down?" Jay squeaked, and managed a grimace.

Voices from below reminded Drew of their peril. "Sshh. Follow me," he whispered, and swung out onto the nearest tree branch.

Jay hesitated. "It's a lot farther down than it looked on the way up." He took a deep breath and stepped carefully into the tree. But his foot slipped and he swung overhand from branch to branch like a monkey, smothering groans and curses.

A blue jay sounded an alarm. Sure of discovery, Drew shrank behind the branches and wished he were green. But instead of a challenge, the next sound he heard was an ear-piercing scream.

"Talk about a bird's-eye view!" he marvelled.

On the path to the girls' outhouse, Hilde Simmons was snivelling into the bodice of another girl. The rest of the girls crowded around the outhouse, pointing at the snake.

Then one of them swung her arm and pointed down the road.

From his vantage point in the tree, Drew spied the teacher's '29 Model A lurching down the road toward them. "Hurry, Jay! Miss Jordan's coming." He paused long enough to watch Jay get his footing on a sturdy branch and begin to pick his way downward.

Drew shinnied the rest of the way down the rough trunk while Miss Jordan parked her car.

Before she could get her door open, there rose a chorus of "Teacher, Teacher," and everyone chattered at once.

Miss Jordan took in the scene at a glance. She smoothed her suit jacket over her hips and began to give orders as she patted Hilde's hand. "Here, you older boys—Gordon, Richard—get rid of that snake." She glanced at the brooch-watch pinned to her lapel and, towing Hilde after her, hurried up the steps to the schoolhouse door.

When she had disappeared inside the building, Drew strolled up to join the knot of boys at the foot of the steps, Jay at his heels. No one even considered going into the school before the bell rang.

Through the open door, Drew saw Miss Jordan yanking on the bell rope. The bell did not ring. He risked a look at Jay.

Jay's face bore battle scars from the tree. Drew stared at the cuts and scratches on his own arms. He ran shaky fingers through his hair and combed out a fistful of leftover twigs and leaves. He brushed and swiped frantically at himself and Jay to destroy the tattletale evidence, but slouched carelessly when Miss Jordan appeared in the doorway.

Richard Price came around the corner of the building. "The snake was already dead, Miss Jordan."

"Thank you, Richard. Now will you please climb up the ladder and see why the bell won't ring." The teacher riveted Drew with a look. Her eyes were as blue as the sky at threshing time.

Gordon Madsen sidled up to Miss Jordan. He stared at the ground. "Drew and Jeremiah did it, Miss Jordan," he whispered. "I saw them put the snake in the girls' privy, and they tied the knot in the bell rope."

Miss Jordan shook her head at Drew and Jay and clucked her tongue. Her eyes clouded. "Isn't it about time you two grew up? Neither of you can get to be the Man of the Year this way."

The bell clanked experimentally and then began to peal. The holdouts straggled into the school's one room.

"Walter Drew Ralston and Jeremiah Justice, please see me after school," Miss Jordan said. She made a ceremony of removing her hat and threading the long hatpin through its crown. "I will have notes for your parents."

Marching like condemned prisoners, Drew and Jay went to their seats in the back row. To avoid the smirks turned his way, Drew stared at the big yellow map of Kansas on the wall. From across the center aisle, he heard Gordie whisper to the other older boys, "The shrimp did it; the shrimp and Jay."

Drew's ears burned and he slumped in his seat. He hated being the smallest eighth grader. He hated Gordie Madsen. Once again he vowed to grow up, to stop this little-boy stuff.

The *tick-tock* of the eight-day Regulator clock, loud in the quiet room, had never seemed so slow. Drew wished he had stayed home to help Dad plant their last hope for a garden. Then he began to dread having to face Dad with a note from the teacher.

He passed the time by trying to decide which he would rather do: remain a prisoner at school, or go home with one of Miss Jordan's notes.

Getting out of this stuffy room would be better, he concluded. Once he got Dad's yelling out of the way, his birthday might yet be salvaged.

CHAPTER **2**

The golden sunlight slanting on Drew's desk seemed to taunt him. Then the light dimmed as if someone had blown out a candle. Drew stared out the window.

Overhead the blue sky still beckoned, but the loveliness of his birthday morning had vanished. A tarnished-brass color stained the horizon. The wind had gone; the elm's new leaves hung motionless.

Miss Jordan lit the carbide lamps. "Seems we're to have a spring storm, boys and girls," was all she said. But something in her tone alerted Drew.

Dust hung in the air between him and the lights. A halo circled each lamp. His heart thudded.

The students shuffled restlessly, and a first grader began to cry.

Drew slid to the window. He scanned the horizon to the south and west but saw nothing. He craned his neck. In the north appeared a towering wall of black. The sides spread outward as it bore down upon them.

But it was no thunderstorm, nor even a cyclone. Worse; a duster.

Drew steeled his voice. "Miss Jordan," he said evenly. "Could you please come here a minute?"

Without seeming to hurry, Miss Jordan stood at Drew's

side in an instant. Tall for a lady, and thin, she seemed scarcely older than Hilde. Her eyes held his.

Drew understood that he should say nothing to upset the younger children. Silently he inclined his head to the north.

Miss Jordan rested a slender hand on Drew's shoulder as she leaned to peer out the window. "Dear God," she barely whispered. She closed her eyes, and her chest rose and fell as she took a deep breath.

Then she turned more calmly than Drew thought possible and pushed back a strawberry-blond finger wave. "Yes," she said, "it seems we're going to have a dust storm." She patted his arm as she left his side.

Drew almost whistled his admiration. No wonder half the sixth graders were in love with her, he thought.

The teacher glided back to the front of the room. "Girls and boys," she said coolly, "let's straighten the classroom. Everyone clear off his desk, please. I'm sure they've announced on the radio. . . . Your parents will be coming for you any moment." She glanced casually around the room. "Hurry, please."

She mounted the dais and put away everything on the top of her desk. Ignoring the confusion at her back, she rolled up maps and put the globe in the cupboard. She draped a towel over the water bucket resting on its bench behind the heating stove. Drew had to watch carefully to detect the trembling of Miss Jordan's hands.

The classroom's uncommon neatness seemed all the stranger in the deepening darkness.

Drew peered out the window. "Here they come, Miss Jordan."

As usual when a duster gave enough warning, a caravan of dirty square cars approached on the gravel road. Rapidly and loosely constructed, the schoolhouse made a poor shelter from a full-fledged dust storm. The building emptied quickly to only the murmur of concerned adult voices.

Jay's father clasped Drew's shoulder. "Need a lift, boy?"

He met Mr. Justice's gaze. "No, sir. It's too far out of your way. I can cut through the woods along the creek and be home in no time."

Jay swiped at the dust beginning to film his glasses. "Sure you'll be okay?" he asked.

"Sure. If Dad didn't think I could make it okay, he'd come after me." Drew hoped his bravado sounded more real than it felt.

He lingered while Miss Jordan locked the building and stomped her flivver to life.

She darted a glance over her shoulder at the ugly cloud of dust bearing down on them. "Drew, why don't you hop in and I'll run you home." Her lip quivered when she smiled.

"That's okay, Miss Jordan. You better go on. You got to go all the way to town, and I just live a quarter mile. I can beat it." He jerked a look at the duster.

"Well, then, don't dawdle." She flashed him a stronger smile and gnashed the gears. With a wave, she guided the car carefully onto the road.

The weird morning twilight swallowed the car quickly. Drew heard its labored chug-chugging long after it had disappeared from sight.

He gazed around him. The landscape had taken on a hazy sepia tone, as though viewed through a brown bottle. No movement disturbed the unearthly calm and stifling heat.

The heavy air smelled and tasted of dust; it gritted between his teeth. His eyes smarted and watered.

For once there was no wind, no wind-whipped particles to cut and sting. He had struggled with the wind all his life, but he missed it now. Better the familiar enemy than the unknown.

"Best get on home," he said aloud. His own voice sounded different in the unnatural silence.

Drew lifted his cap and wiped his sweaty forehead on his shirtsleeve. Every hair on his head stood on end. When he ran his fingers through it, static popped and crackled, and he felt a tingle in his scalp and fingertips. He clamped on his hat and hustled out of the schoolyard.

From the corner of his eye, he sensed a rapid movement—and a kind of flash. He pivoted, but saw nothing. After a heartbeat he forced his feet to move again.

When the path for home took a shortcut across a pasture, Drew sidled along the fence rather than venture into the open. If the black blizzard closed in and blotted out the last of the feeble light, he would need the fence to keep his bearings.

Again the flash. A ball of fire raced along the top wire of the fence toward him, followed quickly by another. He leaped back and stumbled to the ground. He threw his arm across his face and gaped at the fiery balls chasing each other along the fence. The only sound was a faint hiss as each fireball charged along the wire. A sulphurous odor edged out the smell of dust.

He scrambled up, ready to dodge one of the blobs if it chased straight for him. He swallowed hard, aware of the loud knocking of his heart. After a moment he realized the glowing orbs zoomed only along the fence, and he forced his shaky legs into a run.

When he came again to the dirt road where it curved around the pasture, the ball lightning still swooshed along its fence track like a long freight train. But Drew no longer watched it.

When his tennis shoes struck the surface of the road and tossed up a little cloud of dust, it hung in the air. As he crossed the road and scrambled up the bank on the other side, he heard a motor sputtering. He turned and searched the murk. It might be Poke coming home from high school, or Dad's truck.

The lighted headlamps appeared first, like two disembodied ghostly globes. Caked with dirt, the car was the heart of a roiling cloud of dust that followed it along the road. A strange bluish green light, like the tip of a welder's torch, hovered all around the car.

As it passed him, Drew saw the look of amazement on the driver's face. He appeared transfixed by the awful halo surrounding his car. The smell of sulphur grew stronger.

Drew stared around him. The hair on the back of his neck stood up; he felt goosebumps prickle his skin. The sky—the daylight—had been swallowed. Beyond a few feet the rest of the world had been dusted over.

He recalled the stories of how people caught outside, often just a few feet from their doors, became lost in a duster. Some had wandered in the dust until they suffocated. He shuddered and sprinted for the woods.

The ground lifted sharply—the railroad embankment, the firm reassurance of the steel tracks, filling now with dust. Once away from the railroad cut, he strained for a glimpse of his popcorn field at the nearest point of his farm.

He wished he were already home with Mom, who would surely be terrified.

And what about his sheep? Dad had made it plain that the helpless sheep were his own responsibility.

His chest felt tight and every breath came hard. Each footfall churned up a pillar of dust, and running used too much precious air. He slowed to a walk and wiped the grit from his smarting eyes, then tied his handkerchief around his face like a mask.

At last he cleared the trees and could make out his own pasture fence. Wind-driven against the wire, tumbleweeds had lodged in the fence corner and loomed there like dusty monsters. But at least no globs of fire played tag on the fence.

The darkness deepened. He followed the fence all the way to the barnyard. As he passed the chicken pen, he saw that the chickens had gone to roost.

And then he saw the barest glow of lamplight from the house. He longed for the safety of the kitchen, but the sheep were waiting. Fear for their welfare stabbed at him.

Heedless now of the dust he stirred, Drew jogged the rest of the way to the sheep pens, careful to keep the lifeline of fence in sight. Squinting into the darkness, he could not see the sheep. He could scarcely see his hands.

In his haste he fumbled with the wire loop holding the gate and raked his knuckle on a barb. He heard his own raspy panting through the gritty handkerchief, and his pulse pounded in his temples. Perspiration trickled down his sides. He shuddered, the kind of chill he had, Mom said, when someone walked on his grave-to-be.

Still he saw no sign of the sheep. Alarm fluttered inside

him. He had built that flock for five years from a ewe and her lamb that his Uncle Clayton had given him when he was only eight. By paying close attention to Clayton's advice, he had become a good shepherd. Though there were a surprising number of them, considering the poor condition of the ewes, this spring's lamb crop had remained small and weak. But Dad had said, "They're all we've got left that's worth a dime." If he lost them now . . .

Then, dimly, he heard their fearful whimpers. He strained to see. The sheep huddled together in the fence corner, their dirty wool camouflaging them against the landscape.

They milled uneasily as he approached. "Hello, girls, it's only me. I'm here now," he murmured. As always, his voice soothed them. He forced himself to move quietly among them. So much dust in their once-white fleeces, dirt caked on their faces.

He dropped his hand to the nearest ewe and patted her flank. "Come on, ladies, let's head for the barn and a nice cool drink of water." He clucked encouragement.

The sheep bleated nervously and bunched around him. In the dust he could not keep them all in sight at once.

"Just follow each other as usual, okay? And hope that the lambs can keep up."

But which way to the gate? He peered around him, unable to see through the wall of dust between him and the barnyard. In his concern for the sheep he had lost sight of the fence line.

It could be only a few steps away, but if he strayed in the wrong direction, he might wander too long in circles.

Then came the mournful wail of a train, dust-muffled:

two long, one short, one long. Drew spoke to reassure the flock. "Must be the freight to Salina. . . . She's coming to the crossing at the county road."

He cocked his head and listened intently. "There—that direction. Then the gate has to be that way, too."

He buried the fingers of one hand in the leader's fleece. Though he could not see the rest of the flock, he heard their labored breathing and the plop of their hooves in the dust behind him.

Once outside the pen, Drew shuffled in the direction of the barn. Sooner or later he had to hit it if he was going straight. He strained his eyes, expecting momentarily to see its bulk looming out of the dust. For the first time he was grateful that Granddad had prided himself on having built the biggest barn in the neighborhood.

When at last Drew bumped into the side of the barn, he felt along its side to the door like a blind man. The sheep crowded him closely.

Turning thirteen on Friday the thirteenth was very bad luck, Mom had said. But he'd had the good luck to reach the sheep before it was too late. And the train had given him his bearings.

Maybe luck was all in how you looked at it. Or maybe you made your own luck, he thought.

Years of practice in early morning darkness guided his hand to the lantern near the door. More good luck—he still had his matches.

The lantern managed only a foggy glow through the dust, but now he could at least see his feet and a narrow circle around them. The homey smell of the barn almost overcame the stench of dust.

The sheep pushed to the stock tank. A thick layer of dust floated on the surface of the water; it looked like thin mud. But the sheep had already dipped their noses into it gratefully.

Drew frowned and felt his dust-caked forehead crinkle. His knees threatened to buckle. He pulled off the encrusted handkerchief mask and sagged against the rough boards of the barn wall. Weariness sat on his shoulders like a feed sack.

Sliding to a squat, he closed his eyes, just for a moment.

CHAPTER 3

". . . blamed thing won't start. We'll just have to saddle some horses." Close by, Mr. Ralston's angry voice grated with frustration.

Drew blinked gritty eyelids and peered around him. Like a second dawn, a feeble daylight had followed in the wake of the dust storm.

He forced himself erect and wondered how long he had slept. Dad would not be happy to catch him napping, even accidentally.

Shoot, he thought, his father ought to know the old Oakland never ran after a duster. Drew did not bother to cover a yawn and unbent his left leg. Still asleep, it felt as if he had parked it on a cactus.

He gathered himself to rise, but out of the corner of his eye he caught a glimpse of Poke's fist just before it slammed the wall over his head. The side of the barn shuddered, and the sheep started and bleated nervously.

Drew ducked instinctively, lost his balance, and sprawled in the dirty hay.

Poke shuffled through the dust in the doorway and slouched against the barn door. He pushed his felt hat to the back of his head and grinned lopsidedly. "Why, you little sneak! You been loafing around out here while the whole countryside's hunting for you." He coughed and kicked Drew's foot with a dust-caked boot. "Better get out of here, little brother. You got some explaining to do."

He drawled the last over his shoulder, but Drew caught what came next as he scrambled to his feet. "Hey, Dad, call off the search. The runt's been sacked out in the barn all this time."

Drew heard a gasp that could only be Mom's, then a tense silence. He took a deep breath.

"Well, I'll be . . . Drew, get out here!" Dad shouted.

Drew hurtled out the door and collided with Mom.

Fingers still crossed, her hands fluttered over him. "Are you all right?"

"Sure, Mom. I just . . ."

She snatched him to her. "My law, you scared us might near to death. What a childish trick!" But her voice trembled and she clung to him.

"I wasn't playin' tricks. I was so tired after . . ."

With a scowl as dark as the duster, Dad loomed over Mom's shoulder. His eyes seemed to bore into Drew. "You all right, son?"

Drew nodded. He recognized on Dad's face the same panic he had felt when he thought the sheep were lost. He forgot the speech he had improvised on the way out of the barn.

Dad drew a quavering breath. "Ain't you never gonna grow up, boy?" he demanded. "Get to the house!"

"I just—"

"Now!"

"Yes, sir." Drew shrugged and trudged up the dusty path, Mom clucking at his heels.

"Poke, see if you can head off Clayton and the others. They'll have plenty to do at home without a wild-goose chase," Dad said. "Thank God I've got *one* son I can count on not to pull such fool stunts."

Drew glanced over his shoulder and saw his older brother shamble into the barn. He stared at his own feet, shoelace deep in the dust in the path. Arval, the favorite—blameless in their parents' eyes, even though he was lazy and undependable and never around when you needed him. How else could he have wound up with a nickname like *Poke*?

And if he was so perfect, why hadn't Poke run the Oakland into the garage when he got home, as he was supposed to, instead of leaving it out by the barn? Probably in a hurry to read his latest western. All he ever did was lie around and read. Even Mom said that if Poke read as many law books as he did westerns he could be a lawyer.

"Oh, my poor lilac." Mom stopped following him and went to hover over the bush outside the back door. She brushed dust from the few anemic leaves tattering its branches. "I don't see any buds yet. Oh, I do hope the drouth ain't got it." Though there had been no water to spare for purely ornamental plants, she had done her best by the bush, routinely hauling out her dishwater to dump at its base.

Drew shrugged. Granddad's dumb lilac bush even got in the family album—pictures of himself and Granddad standing in front of it on the last day of school every year. Though usually in full bloom by then, the lilac did not look like it would make it this year. Drew knew what to expect next from Mom.

"If this lilac dies, I die with it," Mom said. "That's what the gypsy told me at the fair." She hurried to the pump for water. "Drew, you grab that broom and start sweeping the porch," she called over her shoulder.

The dusty broom leaned against the side of the house where dried, faded yellow paint chips clung here and there. He remembered a far-off time, before the depression, when Mom had been so proud of her bright yellow house.

But hard times and dust storms had scoured it almost bare.

"Poke, you can unsaddle," Dad called from under the hood of the car. He jerked his head toward the lane. "Clayton."

Mom liked to say her brother Clayton would never have a son of his own as much like him as Drew—a lot to live up to. Although Uncle Clayton stood not much taller than Drew, Dad said Clayton was "all man." Now he grabbed Drew in a bear hug.

"Hey, nephew, sure am glad to see you!" he said, his voice a deep rumble. His booming laughter could carry across the prairie, even over the roar of a threshing machine.

Drew followed the grown-ups through the screened-in porch and into the kitchen.

Mom sniffed. "Look at this place." She flung an arm at the room. Dust sifted down the walls like flour in a bin. Despite the rags stuffed around the cracks at the windows, fingers of dust had found their way in around the glass.

"There's even dust in the *icebox*! And the cabinet!" She cleared a swath in the dust on the worktable. Her shoulders slumped, as if worn down and beaten by the dust.

Drew peeked into the pie safe. No birthday cake.

"Sorry you had to make the trip for nothing, Clay." Dad glared at Drew and snatched a wooden chair from the table.

"Think nothing of it, man. I'm just glad the boy's all right." Clayton winked at Drew and sat on the edge of the chair, twirling his hat in his hands.

Dad straddled his own chair backward and held himself tautly erect, his mouth hard and thin. Absently he rubbed the callus on his thumb. "Clay, this duster is just about the last straw. Can't see much hope for rain now."

Drew squatted near the door. If he was to hear the grown-up talk, they would have to forget he was there.

Clayton nodded and watched his hat. "Looking pretty bad, all right," he agreed.

Mom sagged on a chair, her head bowed. "Bad?" she repeated. "Hopeless, I'd say." She swiped at her face with the tail of her apron.

The screen door squawked as Poke came onto the porch. He lifted his wide-brimmed hat and slapped it against his thigh before entering the kitchen. Dust flew, and Poke coughed violently. Although it had been more than a year since he'd caught the flu in the epidemic, he hardly seemed any better.

Dad waited until Poke's coughing subsided, then said, "I've made up my mind. . . . If it don't rain by the Fourth of July, we're pullin' out."

Drew gasped. He lost his balance and crashed into the wall. Dust billowed around him.

"Now you're talking, Dad." Poke pulled a chair away from the table and draped himself across it, tilting it back and balancing it against the wall behind him so that his long legs stretched into the room. His green eyes and sandy hair echoed Dad's and contrasted sharply with Mom's and Drew's coal black hair and dark eyes. Perhaps that explained why Dad had always been partial to Poke, Drew thought.

"Drew, you get to choring," his father said. "This don't concern you."

"Yes, sir." Drew punished Poke with a glare, then went out, catching the screen door before it slammed.

He hesitated on the back steps. He had to know Dad's plan. How could he even think of leaving the farm Granddad had homesteaded, hard won with sweat and blood?

"Well . . ." That was Clayton. He thought and spoke slowly, but his word was his bond. "Lots of folks is leaving. Personally, I think they're getting out of the frying pan into the fire, but a man's got to do what he thinks is right."

"Oh, Clayton," Drew's mother said. "Everything's dried up, no crops . . . stock hungry. And this dust . . ." Her voice caught between sobs. "Eating dust, breathing dust—"

"Yeah, we should have left a long time ago," Poke put in. "We're beating a dead horse here."

"My dad will turn over in his grave," Dad said. "The truth is, Clay, the banker's given me till July first to either pay last year's interest or face foreclosure."

From his listening post on the steps, Drew heard the clock ticking in the silent kitchen and wondered at the meaning of *foreclosure*. He pictured how Dad sat stiffly straight, unable to relax even at rest.

A chair scraped on the linoleum. "I wish I could let you have some more, Walt, but the fact is, I've about run out the string myself."

"No, no. No more," Dad said. "I ain't got a prayer of paying any of it back now. I just kept hoping, you know, *next* year. Hoping it would rain, that we'd get a crop, or at least a garden. But now . . . I've lost hope."

Drew could hear his mother crying softly. "But the gypsy said—"

"Aw, Mom, give it up, will you?" Poke let his chair clomp to the floor.

"Bea, don't do this to yourself," Clayton almost whispered.

Dad cleared his throat. "Only thing we got left that's worth anything is the sheep," he said. "We can probably get enough out of them to get to Missouri. I'll go to Kansas City and try to find work."

"Well," Clayton began, "it appears to me there's already a lot of folks in the city out of work—"

Drew burst through the door. "You can't sell my sheep! You said the sheep are my responsibility." He meant to be calm, grown up. But his voice cracked, making him sound like a whining child. "You wouldn't sell my sheep, would you, Dad?"

Dad's fist struck the table. "You get to choring this minute."

Mom laid a trembling hand on his arm. "Walt, the boy—"

"Son, my back's against the wall. Feeding and sheltering you and your mother and brother are *my* responsibility." Dad gripped Drew's shoulder. "If you've learned anything at all from having those sheep, you know how that feels."

Drew bolted; he did not care if the screen door slammed.

The gray sky had lifted, no longer threatening to blot out the land. The sun hung low, like an orange wrapped in dirty tissue paper.

Dust choked the seared and withered weeds still standing in last year's abandoned garden. Dust rose from the path under his feet. He half expected to look up and see a camel caravan of Bedouins, robed and turbaned, undulating down the township road.

Last year at this time his big worry had been how to buy his own ram to build his flock. Now he had to worry about keeping the ewes. And the farm itself.

He glanced at Granddad's old house, built by his own hands of rough-sawn lumber fastened together with wooden pegs. Once Granddad's pride after years in both dugout and soddie, the old house now sheltered only the family's popcorn.

Drew thought he could almost see Granddad resting in the shade of the big old hackberry tree between the two houses. Granddad had planted that tree.

Except for the woods along the creek, Granddad had planted every tree on the farm. They owed every scrap of cool shade to him. They owed everything to him.

How sad Granddad would be to see the trees dying from the drought, and to know his family was losing the farm. If only Dad had heeded Granddad's warning not to mortgage the farm after his death.

"Some birthday," Drew muttered aloud. Morning seemed a long time ago. He remembered the trouble at school and shook his head. Here they were about to lose the farm, and he'd wasted time on such childish tricks.

He squared his shoulders and plodded through the dust to the barn. Milking made a good time to think. He would think of some way out of this mess. And while he was at it, he would have to think about growing up faster.

CHAPTER 4

The next Friday morning found Drew no wiser. "You got any ideas how to make money?" he asked Jay.

They sat, with Billy Boy, shivering on a fallen log near the place where the railroad tracks sliced through the woods along the creek. The fickle spring wind had shifted around to the north.

Jay leaned his hands on his chunky thighs and studied the dirt beneath his feet. "I hear my mom and dad talking about needing money all the time—"

"I got to earn some money," Drew said. "I bet I've asked every farmer I know if he needs any help. He says, 'Sure do, son, but not the kind you can give me.'"

"My dad says there's lots of people looking for work. And even them with jobs have to take pay cuts sometimes to keep 'em." Jay fondled Billy Boy's ears and avoided Drew's gaze. "Hey, too bad Miss Jordan's dumb Man of the Year award don't pay any prize money."

Drew shrugged. "But you know what? I'd like to win it just to show my dad he's got *two* sons."

"I'm glad I ain't got any big brothers. Baby ones is bad enough." Jay pushed up his glasses.

Drew buttoned his denim jacket against the chill. "Can't tell what Dad sees in Poke. He don't do nothing. He don't go on dates or play baseball or nothing. Just mopes around and reads those westerns and whines about not havin' any future. Boy, if I was getting out of high school in a week, I'd be flying high."

"Rotten luck he can't go to college like he wanted," Jay said.

Drew shook his head. "I don't believe in luck. Bad or good, it's all in how you look at it. 'Sides, Poke just keeps waiting for something to happen. I think you got to *make* it happen!"

"Hey, I thought you was earning money raising sheep."

"Yeah," Drew admitted. "I get a little at shearing time, and then a little more when I sell the lambs. But then that's it till next spring." He jabbed his cold hands into his pockets. "I wish it would warm up again so's I could have the shearer in. I need money now."

Billy Boy left Jay's side and rested his head on Drew's knee. His soft brown eyes seemed to offer comfort and understanding as he cuddled against Drew's leg.

Drew stroked Billy's head, wishing again that Dad would let him have a dog. Every time he asked, Dad said, "I don't need another mouth to feed."

Jay grinned and thumped his fist on Drew's shoulder. "What you need, ol' buddy, is some of your mom's magic."

Drew sighed. "She's been telling me for years how unlucky I am because I was born on the thirteenth. Now she's decided I'm supposed to be lucky 'cause I got a widow's peak." He shook his head. "Women."

"A widow's *what*?"

Drew snatched off his cap. "See how my hair grows down on my forehead to a little point?" He held up the jumbled curls so Jay could see. "That's what they call a widow's peak, and now she says it's supposed to be good luck."

Jay smothered a giggle, and Drew frowned. "If you tell anybody about this, I swear I'll—" He broke off as Billy Boy gave a low growl.

A twig snapped in the woods behind them. Drew whirled in time to see sharp, foxlike features under a red baseball cap disappear into the trees. "It's that Gordie Madsen—spying on us again," he shouted, already in pursuit.

Billy Boy raced ahead of Drew, barking at Gordie's heels. Drew could hear Jay's heavier, slower progress bringing up the rear as they crashed through the trees crowding the path to school.

Though Drew ran as hard as he could, his quarry remained out of reach. By the time Drew and Jay reached the schoolyard, Gordie was panting on the schoolhouse steps, safely near the open door. Billy Boy stood to one side and barked. Drew and Jay pulled up puffing and coughing, their faces red.

Drew spat on the ground. "That danged Madsen—hides behind Teacher's skirt so he won't have to face us."

Jay's face lit up. "Hey, I've got an idea," he whispered. "Play along." He advanced toward the crouching figure, who darted them cornered-fox glances.

"Hey, Gordie, why don't ya come and play with me and Drew?" Jay called.

No answer from the fox.

"Come on, Percy Boy," Drew taunted him.

Billy Boy barked and danced around them, enjoying the game.

"Why don't you leave him alone?" Richard Price called from his post at the edge of the steps.

"Why don't you mind your own business, Price?" Drew returned without taking his eyes from Gordon Madsen's face.

Richard shook his head and turned back to the other boys in his group. The fox sat rock still, as if hoping to be taken for a statue. Even the crafty looks ceased.

"Never mind, Drew," Jay said. "Percy Pants doesn't want to play with us *boys.*"

"Yeah, Gordie is a sissy," Drew singsonged.

Jay joined in and they chanted, "Gordie is a sissy; Gordie is a sissy."

At last Gordie scrambled up, swinging his fists wildly, his face streaked with tears.

Drew laughed and danced just out of Gordie's reach. "Don't ever spy on us again, stool pigeon," he spat when the two were inches apart. He snatched the red cap off Gordie's head and tossed it to Jay.

Cap in hand, Jay disappeared around the side of the school building, Billy Boy at his heels.

Gordie set up a wail that brought Miss Jordan to the door. "All right, Drew, see me after school again." She shook her head and sighed. "Aren't you ever going to grow up? I would think you could be a little kinder to Gordie on his last day with us. I'm remembering all this when it comes time to decide on the Man of the Year. And send that dog home," she flung over her shoulder before disappearing inside the schoolhouse.

Drew winced. Miss Jordan's words lashed like a whip, right on his bare conscience.

Jay came back around the side of the building. "Last day?"

Gordie gave them a martyred look. "We're moving to town to live with my grandma."

"Gee," Drew said, because he could think of nothing better, "I thought you liked living on a farm."

Gordie looked ready to cry again. "But the bank foreclosed. They're having the sale this afternoon." His voice broke, and he sat down heavily on the steps.

The bell jangled its ultimatum. Price and the others trooped inside.

Jay started off, and Billy Boy moved closer to Drew.

"Where you going?" Drew asked. "It's time to go in."

"Jeremiah!" Miss Jordan demanded from the door. "Get rid of that dog and get yourself in here this instant."

"Gee, Miss Jordan, I gotta—" Jay began.

"Jay Justice, I said *now.* I'm losing my patience with you two."

"Go on home, Billy. That's a good dog." Jay hung his head, red faced, and followed Drew and Gordie into the building.

A chill invaded the classroom. It started to snow, a curious mixture of snow and dust, so that it seemed to be snowing mud. Miss Jordan began to lay a fire in the heating stove.

Jay drummed his fingers loudly on the top of his desk.

Drew obeyed the signal and glanced over at him.

Jay circled his throat with his hands like a noose. His tongue stuck out and his eyes bulged.

"What's wrong?" Drew mouthed.

Jay shook his head violently and pointed to Miss Jordan firing up the wood stove.

Drew shrugged and lifted his eyebrows.

Jay's face grew redder. He pantomimed, "I put Gordie's cap down the chimney." He slid down in his seat and watched Drew's face, waiting for a solution.

Drew thought fast. If they said anything, Miss Jordan would know they were guilty—and they were in enough trouble already.

Nothing to do but wait for the show. He shook his head at Jay and pressed his index finger to his lips.

Before long, smoke began to drift through the schoolroom. Intent on writing a lesson on the blackboard, Miss Jordan failed to notice. Behind her, the pupils coughed and rolled their eyes. They waved their arms as if they could push away the gray smoke filling the room. Drew watched Miss Jordan's back and bit his lip to keep from laughing.

At last the teacher whirled from the blackboard. "Oh, dear." She yanked at the damper on the stove, already open wide. Still the smoke poured into the room.

Drew raised his hand. "Miss Jordan, would you like me to fix it? This happens all the time at home." His voice sounded deep and manly; it didn't crack.

Miss Jordan looked hopeful. "Do you think you can?"

Already on his way up the aisle, Drew heard his classmates opening windows and whooping behind him.

Coolly he spread some old newspapers from the kindling box on the floor under the stovepipe. Using his handkerchief as a hot pad, he separated the pipe and peeled Gordie's blackened cap out of the joint.

Drew rolled the smoldering cap into a layer of sooty newspaper and tossed it into the stove. By the time he had replaced the pipe and returned to his seat, the stove had begun to draw properly and the smoke to clear.

"Thank you, Drew." Miss Jordan looked at him with new respect.

Some of the others looked at him with suspicion.

"I'll never forget you for this," Jay said, his glance shining. Drew laughed and held his clenched hands aloft like a victorious prize fighter.

All morning the dusty snow swirled around the schoolyard and blew across the road. Finally Miss Jordan said, "Students, I believe we'll dismiss at noon today." She smiled at the cheer that went up from the classroom.

Drew heaved a sigh of relief. His mother's expression, "It's an ill wind that blows no good," was never truer than when a duster made Miss Jordan forget to write a note to his father.

At home Drew found his mother waging her constant battle with the dust in the house.

Although she had washed the curtains after last week's dust storm and mended them again, they hung limp and ugly amid scarred furniture and linoleum that cracked around the edges. Dusty wallpaper peeled off the wall. "Depression decorating," she called it.

"Tell you what, boys," Dad said when Mrs. Ralston shooed them from the kitchen. "All this hustle and bustle around here makes me nervous." He gave them a wink. "After dinner let's us men go over to Madsen's sale."

Drew's heart lurched. He did not want to go to Gordie's sale, but it probably wouldn't be long before Mom tied an apron around him and put him to sweeping dust.

Instead she smiled at Drew. "You fill that woodbox before you go, you hear?"

Drew nodded.

When at last he escaped into the dreary afternoon, dust and snow still scudded around the outbuildings and across the fields.

Mr. Ralston scanned the horizon. "Ain't gonna amount to much." He shook his head. "God, what I wouldn't give for a good rain."

While Poke backed the Oakland out of the shed, Drew wondered how much longer Dad could keep the old car running without spending money on it. The Oakland was dusty and faded green, ugly even when new. It boasted spiffy spoked wooden wheels. But all four tires were worn out and patched with canvas cut from old tarpaulins. Often they had to stop along their way to patch again.

"Hey, little brother, why don't you drive?" Poke got out from behind the wheel and pushed Drew forward.

Drew shrugged and glanced at his father. His driving practice had not earned him gold stars.

"I don't know, Poke," Dad said. "He can't hardly see over the dashboard."

"Yeah, well, he can sit on this cushion here to make him taller." Poke slipped Dad's hot-weather mesh cushion into the driver's seat and shoved Drew onto it.

Mr. Ralston started to protest.

"Now, Dad, he's got to learn. How's he ever going to learn if you don't let him practice?" Poke slammed the driver's door and sprawled in the backseat.

He always gets his way, Drew thought. How humiliating to have to sit on a cushion! He eased the car into gear and steered cautiously past the barn and the worthless old tractor parked nearby. The worn-out Fordson sat under a tree, while they were forced to use horses for plowing and hauling long after most farmers had switched to trucks and tractors.

Gordie Madsen's father had bought a "new" used tractor just about the time this drought started. Drew wondered if the payments on that tractor, unable to earn its keep, were the final nails in the coffin of Gordie's farm.

His next thought was even worse. Neither were the Ralston horses able to work for their keep in the hard-baked and dusty fields. And, unlike a tractor, they must be fed whether they worked or not.

Drew shuddered. Did his own farm hang by such a slender thread?

CHAPTER 5

Drew drove carefully. To his surprise, Dad did not yell or curse even when the car hit the railroad tracks too fast or when a gust of wind almost jerked the wood-spoked steering wheel from Drew's hands.

Dusty snow powdered the junipers edging the Madsens' lane. It skiffed the windshields of the cars parked there and promised to pile up in the corners of their running boards.

When Drew eased the Oakland in behind the line of cars, Poke patted him on the back. "Good job, little brother."

Dad said nothing.

His heart still hammering, Drew sat behind the wheel a few seconds after the others left. He took a deep breath, as if he had forgotten to breathe while driving, and inhaled the familiar farm smell of straw, animals, and old manure.

He slid from behind the steering wheel and slammed the car door as he had seen Dad and Poke do, then trudged up the graveled lane. Set well back from the road at the head of the lane, the house seemed lonely despite the gathering crowd. A short picket fence separated a small square of yard from the barnyard. Neither displayed even the memory of grass.

Drew scouted for Jay or someone else from school. Trestle tables made of boards on sawhorses displayed the

Madsens' meager belongings. The boards sagged under the weight of cracked dishes, iron skillets, and pickle crocks.

A Victrola cabinet straddled a dust dune in the yard. Imagining his mother's response to such a sacrilege, Drew snatched a ragged quilt from an adjacent sale table and tossed it over the phonograph to protect it from the snow.

Work-worn women with long faces clutched their coats and clustered around the pillowcases and fern stands and butter churns. Some inspected various items carefully. Others just looked, keeping their cold hands in their pockets.

Most of the men were down by the barn, looking over the stock and machinery. The singsong chant of the auctioneer pulled Drew like a magnet. He edged through the knot of men to the inside of the circle, where he could see.

A stone-faced Gordie stood by the auctioneer's clerk, holding a young mule. He appeared to grip the halter more for support than to hold the animal.

"Lookee here, boys," the auctioneer called. "Just what you need—a strong, steady worker. Almost three years old, got a good start, been well cared for, serve you well. What do I hear for this young fella?"

"Who's his dam?" called a man near Drew.

The auctioneer quickly consulted Gordie. Drew did not hear the mumbled reply.

"Smith's Lady Anne—you know her, a fine Belgian mare. Broke to ride, boys. Now, do I hear five dollars, five dollars where?"

"Two bits," the man said, and hitched up his overalls.

"I got two bits, two bits," the auctioneer chanted. "Now

a dollar! Do I hear one dollar, one dollar where?"

"Fifty cents," someone called from the rear of the crowd.

The auctioneer stopped his chanting. "Boys, I don't think you understand what we've got here. You should be begging me to sell you this fine mule colt. Now, my clerk is a horse trader." He turned to the red-faced clerk. "Slim, tell 'em what you told me about this here mule."

Slim's Adam's apple bobbed. "Well, it appears to me he's a mighty fine mule!" He glanced uncertainly at the auctioneer.

"Now, what did I tell you, boys? There's money to be made! Trot him around there, Gordie, so's the boys in the back can see."

A murmur rippled across the crowd. Staring at the ground, Gordie tugged on the mule's halter and circled the group of men. The frigid wind whipped at the brim of his battered felt hat.

Drew remembered the scorched baseball cap in the heating stove at school. "Give you a hand, Gordie?"

Gordie shot him a look, shook his head. Tears brimmed his eyes.

Beside Drew two men hunkered into faded denim jackets. "Don't know why I come to these dang foreclosure sales," one of them muttered. "Can't think of anything I hate worse."

The other nodded and squirted a shot of tobacco juice behind him. "Ain't no fun, that's for sure. Banker ought to have to see this kid's face." He jerked his head Gordie's way, but did not look at him.

Drew could look nowhere else. The tears in Gordie's

eyes reminded him of the morning's mischief. What I wouldn't give to take it all back, he thought.

"All right, boys, the bid is half a dollar." The auctioneer picked up his spiel. "I got a half, a half here, lookin' for one! Now one dollar where? I want one dollar, one dollar!" The words all ran together, a loud gibberish that made it hard for Drew to think.

His cold fingers shook as he tugged his wallet out of his overall pocket. He knew to the penny how much money he had left from selling last year's lambs, but he had to make sure.

Two dollars. Mom had been pestering him to buy some overalls and a new pair of tennis shoes. If he spent that two dollars, there would be no more money until the sheep were sheared. Worse, Dad would kill him if he spent it.

Gordie stared at the ground. Tears dripped off his chin into the dust at his feet.

"One dollar," Drew crowed.

The first bidder had moved closer to the auctioneer and eyed Drew, gauging his impudence. "Buck fifty!"

Drew's mind whirled as the auctioneer chanted on. "Now, boys," he coaxed. "This here mule is a fine strong animal. He'll run you a couple of hundred in a year or two! I got one-fifty, one-fifty, now two dollars! I want two dollars; who'll bid two dollars; two dollars where?" The rise and fall of his voice seemed to hypnotize the crowd.

"Two!" yelled Drew.

The other men craned their necks to spot him.

The auctioneer spun around and pointed at him. "I got two here, I got two dollars, lookin' for three! Now three where?" He licked his lips like a hungry dog.

The first bidder stared at Drew but did not raise the bid.

The auctioneer scanned the crowd; seemed to sense the withdrawal of the bidder. "Going for two dollars . . ." He looked around again, searching the face of the defeated bidder. "Going . . . *Sold*! to the youngster here for two dollars."

He shook his head and moved away. "Dang kids sure in a hurry to grow up these days. Now, boys, lookee here at this good harness. . . ." The knot of men moved a few steps.

Gordie thrust the mule's lead rope into Drew's hand and fled into the barn without a word or backward glance.

The tobacco chewer shifted his wad. "Well, kid, I see you've got moxie!" He trailed after the others.

Drew nodded uncertainly and led the mule to the barn door. He cleared his throat, though he still did not know what to say to Gordie. The mule snorted softly.

At the sound, Gordie pivoted. The dim light in the barn glistened on the tears in his eyes.

"Gordie, I . . . I just wanted to say I'm sorry."

Gordie nodded and swallowed hard. "He was my 4-H project. I was going to make him a champion. . . ." He sobbed.

"Bet you could've, too. He's a beaut. . . . I know how I'd feel if my sheep had to go." Drew knew that would be the worst thing that could ever happen.

Gordie eyed him as though he did not think him capable of such feelings. "Thanks, Drew."

"Look, Gordie . . . I, uh, the reason I bought, uh, Moxie here, is I want to give him back to you." Drew held out the lead rope and forced himself to meet Gordie's eyes.

Gordie made a sound that was half sob, half laugh. "I

can't keep him! They're taking our farm and we're moving to town. I can't keep a mule at my grandma's house! And his name ain't Moxie, it's Jack."

Drew shrugged.

Gordie dashed away the tears. "Thanks anyway, but I had to let him go. We knew he wouldn't bring anything. Who can afford to feed him? But I can't keep him in town."

Drew opened his mouth to speak, but there was nothing to say. He nodded.

"I won't forget what you tried to do." Gordie took a deep breath. "Uh, I better go see if my mom needs me. She's taking this thing pretty hard. She just kept hoping. . . ." He wiped his nose on the sleeve of his jacket, squared his shoulders, and marched from the barn.

Drew watched from the doorway. So this was what *foreclosure* meant. He wished he did not have to witness the death of this farm or Madsen's poor, half-starved animals.

Thank goodness they still had some feed for their own stock, though Dad said every day there would not be enough to see them through the summer with no crop.

He reached out a hand to the mule and stroked his rough coat. With the proper feed, it would be slick. "Moxie suits you better than plain old Jack," he whispered.

Dark, knowing eyes looked into his. The mule flicked his ears and nuzzled Drew's jacket pocket.

"Yeah, who wouldn't like some sugar?" Drew murmured as he rubbed the mule's velvet nose. "Oh, boy, how am I ever gonna explain you to Dad!" He shook his head and led the mule from the barn. He found the clerk and paid his two dollars.

The naked windows of the Madsens' vacated house

seemed to stare in shocked surprise at the scene before them. With the mule at his heels, Drew wandered the barnyard. As he threaded his way through clumps of silent people, he realized the gathering seemed more like a funeral than a sale.

When it felt as if his knees would support him no longer, he collapsed on a bale of hay and huddled into his jacket. Moxie nuzzled his shoulder.

Drew tasted salt and realized that tears were sliding down his cheeks. He knew he could not let this *foreclosure* happen to his own farm.

"Hey, Drew," Jay called from a few feet away. "I thought that was you. What's with the mule?"

Drew leaped to his feet. He lifted his shoulder and ducked his head to wipe his face on his jacket. "I'm going to the car."

He tugged on Moxie's halter and plodded down the darkening lane. The soft plop of the mule's hooves followed.

Jay inspected the mule quizzically, then hurried into step beside Drew. "Mom says this is the most depressing thing she's ever seen."

Drew glanced around in surprise. "Your mom here?"

"She's over there talking to Mrs. Madsen." Jay pointed.

The two women stood together near the hump of the storm cellar. Mrs. Madsen had turned her back to the sight of her neighbors pawing over her household goods. They, in turn, tried to avoid watching her misery.

Mrs. Justice's face was pinched with cold and sorrow. As she clutched Sally Madsen's arm and mouthed words of comfort, she eyed the storm cellar as if longing to take refuge there.

Drew looked away. "My mom's home cleaning house, as usual," he said to change the subject.

Jay grunted. "We're going to Grandma's afterwards. Mom says maybe she can feed us supper. If not . . ." He left the sentence unfinished.

Drew tried again for a happier subject. He saw Hilde Simmons emerging from the outhouse. The ground in front of the door was trampled to mud. She picked her way across it carefully.

"Hilde," Drew called, and waved energetically when she turned to him.

To Drew's astonishment, Hilde flashed him a smile and waved a mittened hand.

Jay pushed up his glasses. "I think Hilde likes you, Drew."

"Sure; I like her, too."

"Naw, I mean she *likes* you." Jay grinned.

"She's taller than me."

"So what?"

Drew didn't answer. There did not seem to be a safe subject to talk about.

He ignored Moxie's protest and tied the mule's lead to the rear bumper of the Oakland. Slumping into the back seat, he leaned his head against the seat and took a deep breath. The old car smelled of dusty felt.

The mud-colored afternoon had shaded into twilight. Drew watched the pigeons wheel over the barn, peel off, and swoop down for a landing in the rafters, where they would roost for the night.

"What's the matter with you, Drew?" Jay squatted beside the car's open door.

"We haven't had any fun in a coon's age. Everybody's so serious all the time."

Jay nodded. "Yeah, what we need is a good laugh."

A stab of car lights claimed Drew's attention. A new Hudson pulled into the lane and parked some distance away from the rest of the dusty, worn-out cars, as though the driver did not want it soiled by being too near the others. Mr. Carlson, the banker, got out, looked around, and sauntered toward the house.

The crowd had bunched around the last table of goods. The auctioneer worked quickly to finish before the light failed.

Drew roused himself to inspect the shiny new automobile. In the quiet of the lane he could hear the pigeons cooing in the barn. "Look, the grille's a checkerboard—and it's even got a radio!"

"Whewee, pretty fancy!" Jay caressed the twin horns flanking the shiny ornament on the hood. "What's this here thing?"

"That's a winged griffin." If there was one thing Drew knew about, it was cars. "They call it their winged mascot." A gust of wind picked up some dust and settled it gently on the gleaming finish.

"Boy, that'll make the banker mad," Jay said.

"He'd sure hate to get his new car messed up, wouldn't he?" Drew whispered.

He smacked his left palm with his right fist. "Buddy, I know how we can have us a good laugh and teach that old banker some humbleness at the same time."

"You mean humility," Jay pointed out. "How?"

Drew whirled back to the Oakland, snatched Dad's flashlight out of the front seat, and took off behind its beam. Jay hurried after him.

In the vacant barn, out of the wind, it felt warmer. Pigeons murmured overhead. Drew flashed the light around briefly to be sure they were alone. The dark, empty stalls seemed haunted.

He grabbed a gunnysack hanging handily over a manger and started up the ladder to the barren hayloft. A flutter of pigeons greeted his arrival.

Jay caught on and scrambled up the ladder behind him. "We gonna get him some 'winged mascots,' huh?"

CHAPTER 6

Catching the pigeons was easy. When Drew shone his light in their eyes, they let themselves be picked up and put right into the gunnysack.

"How many you reckon it'll take?" Drew asked.

Jay considered. "Six or eight ought to be plenty."

When he had eight birds in the bag, Drew sat in the loft and laughed.

"Sshh," Jay cautioned. He carried the pigeon bag to the door while Drew carried the flashlight. "Better douse the light!" he whispered, and pointed.

People with lanterns milled around in the darkness outside, picking up the items they had purchased.

Drew led the way around the barn and down the lane behind the line of evergreen trees that Madsen had planted as a wind-and-snow break.

When they were even with the banker's car, Drew crouched and listened. He could hear a murmur of voices from near the house, and lamplight spilled into the yard. But it did not reach their hiding place, nor did it shine on the car.

He had an awful thought. "What if the car's locked?"

"It won't be," Jay said.

"You hope." The wind blew miniature cyclones in the

dust of the lane. Drew chuckled. Whatever else happened, the banker's car would be just as dusty as all the rest.

"I'm smallest, so I'll go through," he told Jay, indicating the thicket of trees.

Jay nodded. "I'll hand you the sack."

Drew wriggled through the junipers and turned to take the sack of pigeons from Jay. The birds were strangely quiet. "Psst. Jay."

"Yeah?"

"How am I gonna do this?"

"Shoot." Jay sighed impatiently. "Wait a minute. I'm coming around." He crawled the rest of the way down the lane behind the trees, circled around the end, and crept to Drew's position behind the car. Gravel crunched under his feet and he panted audibly. But no alarm rang out, no footsteps approached.

"Here, I'll hold the bag," Jay whispered. He took the gunnysack from Drew. "You open the door, and I'll just dump 'em on the back seat."

Drew's teeth started to chatter from the cold, or excitement. "Okay, here goes." He reached up and gently opened the car door. The dome light flickered.

Jay cheered silently that the door was not locked. He held the gunnysack shut with one hand and, balancing it on the other, stretched it over the backseat. "Get ready to slam the door," he whispered over his shoulder. Then he scissored his arms and upended the bag in one smooth motion.

The dimly lit interior of the car came alive with the beating of wings and the frightened cries of the birds.

Jay jumped out of the way, and Drew slammed the car

door and switched on the flashlight. For a triumphant moment they savored the sight of the bewildered pigeons fluttering inside the Hudson.

Jay collapsed on the ground, laughing.

"Sshh! Think what a look that old guy will have on his face when he opens the door and sees those old pigeons roosting in his backseat." Drew laughed aloud.

"Sshh! Hey, I don't think we better hang around here!"

Drew sobered. "You're right." He dodged along the dark line of trees back to the Oakland and hunkered down in the floor of the backseat. Jay stumbled in beside him.

Behind the car, Moxie brayed and tried to toss his head. The car jerked as the mule tugged on his lead.

There came a rap on a darkened window. Dad's face appeared out of nowhere, his expression clearly disapproving. "What are you two doing in here?"

"Talking," Drew stammered. "Just talking, Dad."

Poke's head bobbed beside Dad's. "Yeah? Well, Jay's dad is lookin' all over for him."

Jay clambered out of the car. "See ya Monday," he called as he escaped into the darkness.

Drew heard shouts of laughter and anger from the direction of the banker's car and could not resist a look. The beam of a flashlight played around the car. He remembered to keep his face straight.

"What do you know about them pigeons in Mr. Carlson's car?" Dad asked sternly.

To buy time, Drew slid out the door and leaned against the cold support of the dusty car. "Who said I knew anything about it, Dad?"

"Answer my question, boy!" his father ordered.

Poke started, "Dad—"

"Keep out of this, Poke," Dad warned. He turned and jabbed a finger at Drew. "Answer me!"

"Dad, wait a minute," Poke said.

Out of the corner of his eye, Drew saw the banker's new car bumping onto the road. Its headlights danced in its own shroud of dust. He stifled a whoop.

Poke coughed, but pressed on. "I saw a couple of *little* kids do it, Dad. While I was standing on Madsen's back porch waiting for you."

Dad turned to Poke. "You sure about that, son?"

"Yeah. Drew and Jay are eighth graders. They wouldn't do something that silly."

Drew faced his father. Surely Dad could hear the irony in Poke's voice. He might as well confess. "Dad, me and Jay—"

"Yeah, we know," Poke cut in. "You and Jay was over there flirting with that cute little Simmons girl."

"That's enough!" Dad's voice was steel edged. "You two ain't gonna make me forget about that damn mule!" He jerked his head at Moxie.

The mule almost blended into the darkness. He seemed to await Dad's explosion docilely.

Drew shivered and told himself it was the cold. Now came the moment of reckoning—time to trot out all the arguments he had thought up in favor of owning a mule. He tried to make his face plead.

"I hear you blew two dollars for that," Dad said.

"Dad—"

"That money would have bought you a new pair of overalls. And shoes. You're pert near running around in rags, and you up and throw away two whole dollars." Mr. Ralston threw up his hands.

"Dad, he's a real good mule! His dam was Mr. Smith's Lady Anne." Drew's words tumbled out, eager to be heard before Dad's anger cut them off. "He's gonna be a real good worker, once I get some weight on him and—"

"And I bet he's got a real good appetite, too! Just what do you think we're going to feed him? We can hardly feed the stock we got left, and you go and take on something like that." He leaned against the dusty car and shook his head sadly.

Beyond him Drew saw their neighbors still loading cars and trucks in the lane. A few eyed them curiously.

Dad was not finished. "Here you been yammering about wanting to save the farm—stay on the farm—that's all I ever hear from you," he yelled. "Then you go and pull a dumb fool stunt like this."

An onlooker took a few steps in their direction. "Everything all right there, Ralston?"

Dad shot a glance over his shoulder. "Yeah, Charlie." He waved a hand but did not smile. "See you at the stock barn tomorrow."

"Sure, Walt. 'Night." The man moved away.

Drew worked to keep a poker face. The livestock sale? Was Dad going to sell his sheep tomorrow?

Dad jerked a thumb at Moxie. "The mule goes to the sale tomorrow, boy."

Drew gasped. "Aw, Dad, mules are stronger than horses—and they stand the heat better—and they're smarter, too." He risked a look at his father's face, then rushed on. "They hear and see better than horses—and don't need as much water—"

"Don't lecture *me* about livestock, boy!" Mr. Ralston lifted his cap with a shaking hand and resettled it firmly. Even in the dim light, Drew could see that the angry red of his face nearly subdued his freckles. "I doubt if there's any hope I can get rid of the dang thing, but he goes to the sale tomorrow." He turned to the car door.

"Dad . . ."

His father pivoted and jerked Drew by the jacket. "I said he goes to the sale and that's final." He shoved Drew away from him. "Now you get the pleasure of walking your precious mule home in the dark . . . and not another word out of you." His tone warned he meant it.

"Yes, sir," Drew murmured around the lump in his throat.

Poke coughed. "Reckon I'll just keep my little brother company, Dad."

Dad shot Poke a look. His face seemed to sag, and the distant lantern light cast craggy shadows. "Suit yourself. If you'd rather traipse home in the cold and dark than ride . . ." He jerked open the driver's door and climbed stiffly behind the wheel. "Get that animal off my car!"

Drew leaped to obey. He steadied the mule with his touch.

Dad watched through the oval back glass until they were clear, then gunned the old car's engine and ground the gears. The Oakland lurched into the night while the dust of its leaving hung in the air.

Drew took a quavering breath. "Gosh, Poke, thanks a lot."

"Yeah. Well, little brother, I gotta admire your moxie." Poke shuffled down the lane. "Come on, might as well get started." He turned up his collar and jammed his hands into his pockets. Drew laughed and fell into step.

Moxie followed closely, the lead rope slack.

"Ain't he pretty?" Drew said.

"Huh? Oh, the mule? Well, wouldn't say he was pretty, but handsome—maybe."

Away from the empty house, the night seemed less forbidding. The clouds had parted, and a full moon shed so much silver light that it cast their shadows as they paced along the road. Its beauty contrasted sharply with the ugliness of the day. Like a harvest moon, Drew thought, as if there would be any harvest. But he prized the sight of that enormous moon hanging in the tree branches like a lantern. He was almost surprised and somehow comforted to know the world still turned and the moon still rose.

"Hey, little brother, don't you know Mom says it's bad luck to look at the moon through the trees?"

Drew shrugged. He had been right about Dad's jawing. All for nothing. After tomorrow, Moxie would be gone.

"Say, Poke . . . What does *moxie* mean, anyway?" Poke had been the second person to talk about moxie, and Gordie had said the mule's name was Jack.

Poke lifted an eyebrow. "Uh . . . courage, I guess. You know—guts."

They neared the railroad crossing. "Train's coming," Poke said.

Even as he spoke the engine wailed its crossing warning. No barrier protected the dusty country road. The train's headlight split the night, seeming to search out the dust dunes drifted to the fence top. A lighted passenger car swayed past them.

Drew stared back at the blur of faces within. They'll probably say they saw a couple of dumb farm boys, leading a skinny mule in the dark and the dust, he thought.

"Wish I was on that train," Poke muttered huskily. "It's hopeless here. Dad knows that. That's what's making his fuse so short these days."

Drew lifted a shoulder. "This is our home, Poke. We gotta hold on." He studied Poke's face in the moonlight. In some ways it looked as old as Dad's.

The *click-clack* of the train wheels on their tracks seemed to echo: *Hold on . . . hold on . . .*

"Poke, why did you cover for me and Jay with Dad?" Drew almost yelled to be heard over the passing train.

"Well, say—us guys gotta stick together." Poke clapped Drew on the shoulder. "Besides, I figured I owed you one after the other day—when we all thought you was lost and I said you'd been asleep in the barn all along. Later I saw the sheep and I figured out why you was so tired." He flashed his lopsided grin; his teeth gleamed in the moonlight.

Drew felt his face flush hot. "Then why in heck didn't you tell Dad?"

Moxie shied and tried to move away from the train. He lifted his nose and complained loudly. The dimly lit caboose lumbered past, and Drew led his mule across the tracks.

Drew bit his lip. Poor Moxie. The mule would no sooner learn to trust him when he would let him down.

Poke almost collapsed in a fit of coughing. The noise of the train had faded into the dusty moonlight before he answered. "You know Dad don't like being told he's wrong." Again the lopsided grin.

But Dad seemed to have forgotten his anger by the time

Drew finished choring and waddled into the kitchen with a full bucket of foamy milk hanging from each hand.

Dad bent over the bridle he was mending. The reins snaked around his chair. A coal-oil lamp cast a circle of light on the table.

Surprised they had waited supper, Drew inhaled the welcome aroma. An iron skillet full of side meat sizzled on the stove top. The graniteware coffeepot perked cheerfully on the back burner. A bean pot bubbled quietly, filling the room with a tantalizing smell and steaming up the windows.

Mom smiled and patted Drew's cheek. She slid a pan of cornbread into the oven, wiped her floury hands on her apron, and pushed back her hair. A smudge of flour grayed her temple. "You got time for a spit bath, sweetheart."

Dad looked up with a smile and a wink.

"Okay—I can take a hint." Drew carefully lifted the steaming teakettle off the stove and half-filled the washbasin. The pitcher pump at the sink was worthless since the cistern had gone dry. All water had to be carried from Granddad's first well in the barnyard.

"Poke, you got your lessons done?" Dad shot him a glance.

"Yeah, for all the good it's gonna do me," Poke said. "Don't know why I bother. Can't even get a job."

Mom pushed another stick of wood into the stove. Long practice made her movements deft and efficient. She looked like a dancer dipping and pirouetting, bending and stretching as she prepared the meal.

She interrupted the dance to dab at her flushed face with the tail of her apron. "Walt, I wish you wouldn't call Arval by that silly nickname. He's a young man now, about to graduate high school. And you"—she jabbed another piece of cook wood at Drew—"it's bad luck to change a horse's name."

"Mom, he's a mule, not a horse." Drew risked a look at Dad.

Intent on his repair work, Mr. Ralston licked his lips in concentration. He seemed happiest doing the simple things, Drew realized, the old things he understood. Born and raised in the old ways of farming, right here on this farm, he did not grasp the changes that tractors—and the depression—were bringing.

Dad spoke without looking up. "I was out to the granaries and the silo today. We just can't feed another mouth, son."

Drew eyed his father in the cracked mirror over the washstand. "Dad, what about my wool money?"

"Don't start it again." Dad's finger jabbed the air. "He's going to the sale tomorrow and that's final."

Drew stared at the towel in his hands. Even though the sheep were not in their usual good condition, the wool still ought to bring thirty-five cents a pound. He tried to figure how much stock feed the proceeds would buy.

Mom picked at the hem of her apron. "But, Walt, can you get a good price for the mule?"

Dad sighed. "It doesn't matter, Bea. If I get anything for him, it'll be a better bargain than feeding him for nothing. Thanks to the drouth, I've no fields to plow or plant. . . ."

"Maybe we could use him anyway," Drew's mother said. "Mules is supposed to have a real good sense of direction. Maybe it would be a good idea if Drew rode him to school. You know, so's he wouldn't get lost in a duster."

"Mother, the mule is going to the sale in the morning. I don't want to hear another word from either one of you." Dad's voice was flat; his eyes locked Drew's in the mirror. "Unless you want to trade your sheep to save the mule."

He scraped back his chair and stood up. "The banker says . . ." He dropped his gaze. "Not only are we out of money, we're out of time."

In the hushed kitchen the teakettle whispered on the stove. A gust of wind rattled the window; the house seemed to shudder.

"Son." Dad's tone seemed softer, as did his eyes on Drew. "We're eatin' the wool money." He lit a candle and left the room, his head bowed.

CHAPTER **7**

Drew's eyes jerked open to the blackness of his room. What had awakened him? He strained to listen.

Only the sounds of a Kansas night—half-starved crickets, a lonely dog, dust sandblasting the window glass. The house creaked in a south wind.

Then the train whistle—sharp, short, angry: something on the tracks.

He shuddered, snuggled deeper under the comforter.

The jangle of the alarm jolted him awake. By the time he found the clock in the darkness, the angry bell had run down.

He fumbled for his candle and managed to light it without forsaking the warmth of the bed. Its glow flickered on the homemade wardrobe and the orange crate that doubled as chair and nightstand.

When he snagged his overalls off the foot of the iron bedstead, his movements fanned the candle flame and it burned brightly. A huge shadow danced on the wall as he squirmed into his tennis shoes.

Behind the door a hook held so many articles of clothing that it looked like a hunchback lurking just outside the reach of the dim light. Drew undraped his shirt.

He cupped his hand around the candle flame and tiptoed

past Mom and Dad's bedroom. Once downstairs he abandoned all efforts to be quiet. Nothing would wake Poke.

As Drew approached the gun rack on the dining room wall, the candlelight revealed Dad's boots standing by his desk. Crusted with dust, the leather molded to the shape of Dad's legs, the boots seemed almost to embody the ghostly presence of his father. Drew held one of his own feet against a boot and grinned.

The candle glow flickered on a page of his father's open daybook. Drew hesitated, then decided that the journal of farm happenings was not like a private diary. He lifted the candle and read Dad's practiced penmanship:

April 20. Little snow. Foreclosure sale at Madsen's—Drew got a good mule for $2. Stock feed very low. Will have to shoot all but milk cows and sell sheep.

Drew had to steady the trembling hand holding his candle.

Peeling back the blanket shielding Dad's shotgun and Poke's rifle from the dust, he pocketed some shells from the small drawer under the gun rack.

The kitchen still smelled faintly of last night's cornbread and beans. He paused to get a drink from the enameled white dipper in the water bucket. The water tasted dusty.

He jerked his jacket off its hook behind the door and stretched it on. It barely buttoned; the sleeves ended some inches before his arms did. He shook his head and clapped on his cap. Might have to give in and accept Poke's old coat.

In the corner Drew's vintage Marlin, a long-ago present from Granddad, gleamed in the candlelight. He cradled the rifle in his arms and pinched out the candle.

Still high and generous with her light, the moon illuminated the dust being rearranged by the wind. But as he moved away from the house, Drew saw a narrow gray crack opening on the eastern horizon.

Though he had tried to keep out thoughts of Moxie, they crowded in. He wished he could explain to the mule that getting sold beat getting shot. Dad would be mad that he would not be home in time to help with the loading. But that would be like betraying a friend.

Nobody could object to his going hunting on Saturday morning. Now that the pork was almost gone, Mom had been rationing it. Dad would not butcher again unless forced to. He said if they ate their brood hogs, they could not replace them.

But Dad and Poke had been forced to kill the last two litters because they could neither grow nor buy the feed to fatten them, Drew remembered. And the litter before that, although raised to market weight, had been destroyed because no one could buy them. Drew wondered for the hundredth time how grown-ups could let such a thing as a depression happen.

As he neared the woods, the moonlight seemed less bright in the graying dawn. A shadow swept toward him out of the trees, brushed against his face, and screamed in his ear.

Only a screech owl, but it made his heart pound and his knees rubbery. Even so, screech owls were not as scary as hoot owls, whose giant wings swooping through the darkness had sent him sprawling more than once.

The owls had gone to roost in full daylight when Drew

turned wearily homeward across the withered fields. He had seen no game. The few surviving wild creatures were no doubt as hungry as he.

A flicker of movement in a clump of dry weeds up ahead caught his eye. He brought his rifle to the ready and slipped off the safety.

Hardly daring to breathe, he stared at the weeds swaying slightly in the wind despite the dust anchoring them to the ground. Nothing else moved.

Drew spat his disappointment and lowered the rifle.

Then a skinny rabbit broke from the cover of the weeds and zigzagged for the trees, its rapid motion almost a blur.

Drew swung the rifle around and shot from the hip.

The rabbit jerked as if at the end of an invisible tether and dropped. One less rabbit to starve to death.

Drew exulted as he trotted to retrieve his kill. Once again there would be meat on the table, thanks to him. But it seemed that no matter how hard he tried to be a man, everyone still thought of him as a child.

No more kid stuff, he promised as he trudged homeward. Maybe if Dad saw him shouldering a man's share of the work, he would stop thinking about leaving the farm.

As he approached the barnyard, he saw that in his absence Moxie had indeed been loaded into the old truck. Flecks of lather still stood on the mule's wet flanks. Dad and Poke must have had quite a fight getting him into the bed of the truck. Brave and plucky Moxie, true to his new name.

Drew quickly averted his eyes and carefully planned his movements so as to avoid seeing the mule hanging his head over the stock rack.

After leaning his rifle against the rough boards of the washhouse, Drew skinned and dressed the rabbit. Rather than take it into the warm kitchen, he hung it by a hamstring over a nail under cover of the aluminum roof of the washhouse.

He paused at the woodpile and saved himself a trip by taking in an armload of split wood as he went.

His mother was shaking down the ashes in the fire box on the cookstove. Then she banged back a lid to throw in some corncobs. Kept in a special box behind the stove, cobs burned rapidly and hot and made good kindling. The stove cracked and popped as it heated up again.

A coal-oil lamp flickered on the worktable. Mom pulled her shawl close around her shoulders and hovered over the stove.

Drew dumped his load of wood and grinned at Mom. "Got a rabbit." He warmed his hands at the stove.

She smiled. "That's good. I'll fry it for dinner. If I eat one more piece of pork, I'll squeal."

He laughed and endured her tousling his curls.

Mom studied him a moment. "Drew, you should wear that old coat of Arval's. Maybe you can get a little more wear out of it." She yanked it off its hook and held it against him.

"Aw, Mom. I don't want to wear Poke's old stuff."

"Beggars can't be choosers." She eyed him severely. "Use it up, wear it out; make it do, or do without!"

Drew shrugged. Next he must pump a bucket of water to get his mother started in the kitchen. He smiled at the box of kittens yawning behind the stove. Sometimes the box held a sick chicken, an orphaned lamb, or some injured wild foundling Mom was nursing back to health.

She looked up from the flour bin. "Did you notice any buds on the lilac bush?"

"Gee, Mom, I never noticed." He wished he could say he had seen blossoms on the old bush. Mom could use a strong dose of hope, too.

"Getting so late in the spring and still no buds. . . ." She turned to ladle water into the teakettle.

Drew headed for the barn and his chores. A rooster crowed sleepily. The hogs argued over the few ears of corn in their pen.

Moxie called to him from the ancient truck near the corral.

Drew's heart seemed to turn over, but he knew Dad would allow no more argument. He ignored Moxie's pleas and hurried into the barn.

A cow blinked her liquid brown eyes and lowed, impatient to be milked. Dad and Poke were forking hay into the mangers.

"You're late," Dad said.

"I got a rabbit." He tried to sound matter-of-fact.

Dad made no response, but Poke said, "See, Dad, I told you. Drew's growin' up at last. First thing you know, he'll be Man of the Year!"

"Huh? Man of what?" Dad scooped manure out of Rose's stall.

"Man of the Year. The teacher's giving an award at the end of school." Poke chuckled and leaned on his pitchfork.

Dad lifted an eyebrow at Drew.

"It don't amount to much. We were talking about President Roosevelt, and Miss Jordan said he was *Time* magazine's Man of the Year. Somebody said we ought to have our own Man of the Year, and Miss Jordan thought it was a good idea." Drew reached his watering bucket down from its peg.

"Are you running?" his father asked.

Drew turned to a feed bin and managed to avoid Dad's eyes. "Dad, you don't 'run' for it. Miss Jordan and her committee will name the winner on the last day of school. Besides, there's only nine eighth graders."

Dad stared out the door at the dust-choked barnyard. "I just hope we can hold on till school's out. Feed's about gone. Cellar's almost empty. . . ." He shook his head. "Truth to tell, that banker may be doing us a favor. Don't see that we got much choice anyway."

"You're right, Dad," Poke drawled. "We're fighting a losing battle here. Let's give it up and start fresh somewhere else."

Drew took a deep breath, ignoring the taste of dust. "No!"

"Look, son," his father said. "You think I want to see your mother stand there like Sally Madsen and watch what little she's got carried off? Think I want to see Carlson drive his big Hudson roughshod over the land my own father homesteaded?"

Poke coughed in the silence that followed Dad's speech. "Whew! I'm getting out of here."

"My sheep ain't smelly!" Drew called after Poke, despite his awareness of their odor seeping from the lean-to shed nailed onto the side wall of the barn. Dad grunted and trailed up the path after Poke.

Drew lit a lantern to chase the shadows into the corners

of the cavernous barn. He pumped water for the sheep, the chickens, and the cows, then doled out their feed.

He pushed Millie to one side to make room for himself in her stall, then settled down on his three-legged stool to milk while the cow breakfasted. Millie chewed softly and swished her tail in Drew's face. The barn cats gathered in the circle of light from the lantern.

He leaned his head into the cow's side and breathed in the moist warmth of the foamy bucket. He liked to hear each stream of milk hit the bucket with a slightly different sound. A sharp metallic *ping* at first, then a liquid *splash;* then, when nearly full, a voluptuous *guggle.*

Surely Dad must be pleased about the rabbit even if he did not say so. Just once he would like to hear his father say, "Well done."

Drew aimed a stream of milk directly at the face of one of the cats. She quickly zeroed in on the squirts of milk and opened her mouth. Ignoring the splatters, she concentrated on filling her belly. He made the rounds of the cats one by one, and each had its warm breakfast.

"Hey, little brother," Poke called from the running board of the truck, where he rode until the barnyard gate had been closed. "You going with us to the stock sale?"

Without turning to look, Drew said, "Naw, guess not."

When he heard the old truck's *chuckle-chuckle* as it headed down the lane, he went to the door for a last look at Moxie. Catching sight of him in the doorway, the mule tossed his head and brayed.

Drew sagged on a bale of hay and studied the cats as they cleaned their faces and bibs of leftovers.

After a time the pungent smell of woodsmoke wrinkled

his nose. He turned on the hay bale and peered at the house around the edge of the barn door.

Dark, heavy smoke belched from the kitchen chimney. Mom must have left the damper wide open, as if she had meant to send smoke signals.

A quick movement at the back door caught Drew's eye. He squinted to see through the smoke and the porch screen.

Was that a man with Mom?

Drew leaped to his feet, then thought to stay out of sight. He dove inside the door and peeked around it.

A tall man stood behind Mom, one arm circling her waist. In the sunlight something glinted in the man's hand. *A knife?*

Drew stared, his anger turning to fear.

CHAPTER **8**

Drew tried to stay calm as he weighed his options.

If he charged across the barnyard to the house, he would surely be taken prisoner, too.

He might run to Uncle Clayton's for help. But it was too far and would take too long.

If he saddled Rose, the man with Mom would see him ride out. Even if he led the horse out the back door, there was no way to get from the barn to the lane without crossing a large open space. The intruder might spot him and hurt Mom.

But he could not sit idle, like a frightened child, when Mom was in danger.

If he could make his way around the house to Poke's bedroom window, he might get inside without being seen. But he would need a weapon.

He searched the barn. A pitchfork was too long and awkward; the man would grab it away. He needed a club, like a stick of wood. Could he get to the woodpile without being seen?

He darted a glance at the house. The figures were no longer on the porch. Since the smoke curling from the chimney seemed more normal, no doubt they had moved to the kitchen and Mom had reset the stove damper. But the kitchen window faced the woodpile. He could be spotted the moment he left the barn.

Dad and Poke might not be home until noon. The still-slanting sun rays meant three or four hours until then. And the sunlight looked hazy. If a duster blew in, no telling when Dad could get home.

A barn cat rubbed against Drew's leg. He moved impatiently and tried to ignore the rustle of a rat in a dark corner.

The tired moan of a train carried across the pasture. The man might be a tramp off a train. Maybe he had jumped off when the long uphill pull out of the creek bottom forced the train to crawl.

Then Drew remembered the something-on-the-tracks signal before dawn. The fellow probably got off while the train was stopped and hid in the woods until he saw Dad and Poke leave. There would be no reason to worry about a little guy like him.

Hoboes had been to the house before, and Mom fed them when she could. But they had never caused trouble like this. Drew guessed there must be good and bad hoboes, just like everybody else. Or maybe the man was crazy.

What would Dad do? Or Poke, even? If only he had his rifle.

He remembered his marksmanship of the morning, the rabbit hanging in the washhouse. And the rifle . . . leaning against the wall. His heart leaped.

Squinting through the cracks in the barn boards, he tried to measure the distance to the washhouse. Even if he could make it without being seen, how could he get a shot at the tramp?

If he had the rifle, he might get into the house through Poke's bedroom window, then hold the man off until Dad got home.

He scurried around the wall to the back door of the barn. No one was in sight, but the man might be watching from the kitchen window.

The knoll would hide him all the way to the washhouse if he stayed low. Besides, the tramp knew he was around somewhere, and was probably not much worried.

Darting from the cover of the barn, Drew ran stooped over like a movie cowboy. Halfway to the washhouse, he dropped to the ground to reconnoiter. He lay panting and listening for sounds from the house.

A sheep said *baa,* a rooster crowed. From far off over the fields he heard the bray of a hungry mule. With a stab he remembered Moxie.

He peeked up through some weeds. When he saw no movement at the house, he rose slowly to his knees. He glanced at the washhouse to gauge his direction and then sprang up and took off in a broken-field dash.

Relief flooded over him when he stumbled through the open door of the washhouse. He listened but heard no sound from the house.

He blinked his eyes to hurry their adjustment to the gloom of the shack. Impatiently he groped along the rough wall where he had left the rifle. It was not there.

Drew fell to his knees and pawed the dirt floor. *Gone.* The hobo had found it.

Silently Drew cursed himself and pounded his knees with his fists. How many times had he been told to clean his rifle after firing it?

He peeped through a hole cut in the wall for light and air. It did not seem so far to Poke's window from here. He tried to remember if Dad's shotgun and Poke's rifle were in the gun rack this morning. He pictured the rack in his mind as it was when he got the shells.

The smell of frying rabbit reached his nose. His stomach rumbled.

The guy was probably eating in the kitchen, Drew reasoned, with his back to the dining room. He would be facing the back door, expecting someone to come in that way.

If only he could get into Poke's room through the window, he could sneak into the dining room and grab a rifle. Then just around the corner into the kitchen and . . .

But what if the hobo was not in the kitchen? Drew realized that he might pop out of Poke's room right into the enemy's arms. Or find himself looking down the barrel of his own rifle.

He turned to the semidarkness of the washhouse behind him and scanned the dirt floor for a weapon. The wood for the stove where Mom heated the wash water would have to do. He seized a likely looking chunk, tested its heft and balance, then discarded it for another.

Suddenly aware of the uncertainty of his chances for success, he hesitated. But the tramp might hurt Mom. He had to try.

He peered out the window to plan his route. From the washhouse to the granary, then the silo, behind the windmill. He would keep low in case the tramp was looking. And he would not think about getting caught.

He crouched and broke from the washhouse, running, head down, for the granary. It seemed a long way to the little hut, but at last he collapsed beside it, panting. Though usually he could run a long time without getting winded, fear robbed his breath.

Now the silo. He glanced up, got his bearings, then sprang up and ran, reaching out for ever longer strides from the doubled-over position. He glanced at the house, stumbled on a gopher mound, and took several broken steps to recover. He prayed the invader would be watching the lane and the road, not the barnyard.

Drew sprawled behind the windmill platform to catch his breath, stretching out flat on the ground, his head on his arm. His throat was tight and his chest hurt. His heart was pounding; he could hear it.

The windmill platform, on a balmy spring morning such as this, was one of his favorite places to bask in the sun and dream about the long summer stretching ahead. Freedom from school, projects of his own . . .

The vanes over his head creaked in the wind. Round and round they raced. "Be a man," they seemed to squawk. "Be a man."

He scrambled up and sprinted for the house. Though it was not far, the barnyard seemed a vast no-man's-land. He half expected an angry challenge, the whine of a rifle bullet.

When at last he gained the corner of the house, he knelt under the kitchen window. As he panted he gripped his club tightly to keep his hand from trembling.

He crouched to move under the windows along the side of the kitchen and dining room. He heard the murmur of voices in the kitchen and froze.

"You can't get away," his mother was saying. "My other son is choring. When he's done, he'll come in." Her voice sounded scared, though her words were cold.

Then a voice with a sneer. "Yeah, I seen your other son. He's nothing but a little bitty boy. I ain't afraid of him." A snorting laugh.

"Please believe me. We don't have any money—or anything else," Mom said. "If we did, do you think we'd live like this?"

Drew clenched his teeth. Now that he knew the tramp was in the kitchen, he pictured a clear path to the gun rack. He began to move again. Next stop, Poke's window.

But in the next instant he sprawled headlong. The shock and the fall knocked the breath from his lungs audibly. He lost his grip on the stick of wood, and it thumped against the house.

He had tripped over the drainpipe sticking out of the wall from the icebox. As the ice melted, the water ran through the pipe and dripped onto the ground.

He groaned and struggled to his knees on the moist earth.

Overhead the window opened abruptly. "Well, well, what have we here?" the ugly voice grated. "Oho, Mama's big brave hero."

The intruder grabbed Drew by the collar and one arm and dragged him through the window. "Figured it was about time you showed up, bumpkin. Get yourself in here where I can watch you."

Drew looked up into an unshaved, dirty face. He kicked out, flailed with his fists. "You stink!" he shouted.

The tramp snorted, holding Drew at bay with a stiffened arm. The other hand gripped Dad's shotgun. "Want a dose of buckshot, half-pint?"

Drew knew it was futile to continue to struggle, but he glared hatred at his captor.

"That's better. Now get your butt over there." The man jerked his head to the stove. "Your mama will be so glad you've come to rescue her." His cackle of laughter sickened Drew.

Mom's eyes were wide in her white face. "Drew, baby, are you all right?" She swept him into her arms.

"Mom, are you okay? Did he hurt you?" As he returned her hug, Drew darted a glance around the room, hoping to spot his own rifle.

Then he saw that it leaned against the wall behind the intruder's chair.

"I'm all right," Mom answered. "I was just so worried about you, so afraid you'd do something foolish." She held him at arm's length to smile at him. "And you nearly did."

The tramp riveted Drew with a watery stare, then laid Mr. Ralston's shotgun on the table near his half-empty plate. "That's good; stay over there where I can keep an eye on you both while I finish my Hoover pork."

He pulled the chair away from the table and moved Drew's rifle into arm's reach, then sat without taking his eyes from Drew. "Then we'll go treasure hunting."

A grimy hand pawed at the plate beside him, closed over a piece of fried rabbit. He gnawed at it like a starving coyote Drew had once seen in the fields. "Don't like bein' bothered when I'm eating," he said, displaying half-chewed rabbit and a row of broken, decaying teeth. "Last time I ate was in Chicago, and I'm hungry."

Drew stared. The man had no shoes. A pair of holey four-buckle overshoes covered his feet. A wheat sack served as shirt, with holes cut for his head and arms. His white seaman's cap and his trousers were almost coal-black with soot and dirt, and his stench was as ugly as he.

Worse, the wild look in the man's eyes told Drew his hunch was right. The hobo was crazy. And desperate.

"What you starin' at, hick?" More quickly than Drew's eye could follow, the man whipped out a razor. "You give me any trouble and I'll hurt your mama, hear me?"

He motioned Mom to the table and shoved her into a chair near him. "Keep me company, here, Mama. I don't like the look in your little boy's eyes. He might try somethin' stupid."

He waved the razor at Drew. "Just remember, rube—if you get brave, your mama gets this!"

Drew folded his arms across his chest and leaned against the worktable. He scanned the kitchen, looking for an opportunity, a weapon. Reaching his rifle or the shotgun was clearly out of the question. A smelly thing draped over a chair in the corner must be the man's coat. Now stained and spotted like a leopard skin, it had been a yellow camel's hair overcoat.

He forced his gaze back to the table. Her hands in her lap—fingers crossed—Mom sat stiffly on the edge of her chair, staring at the floor.

Got to do something, Drew thought. *But what?* He jammed his hands into his jacket pockets. His fingers closed on objects that were round and smooth.

He fingered them. The extra rifle shells from this morning. If only he had some way to explode them.

The cooling cookstove popped, loud in the quiet room.

Drew stiffened. Only an arm's length from the stove, he casually edged toward it.

"Here, hero, what do you think you're doing?" The sneer said the tramp was not worried.

Drew jerked his head at the cookstove. "Fire's cooling off. Just gonna stoke it a little."

But somehow he had to get Mom away from the shotgun and the razor. He pretended to glance idly out the window behind him. "Hey, look, Mom—buds on the lilac bush."

Before the man could react, Mom leaped to her feet and flew to Drew's side. "Oh, where?"

As she neared him, Drew grabbed her. With the other hand he yanked down the door of the fire box and tossed in the rifle shells.

As he pivoted, he saw the hobo advancing on them, the razor in one hand and the shotgun in the other.

Drew threw his weight against his mother, using his forward momentum to push them both away from the stove.

Suddenly they seemed under fire. The exploding shells rocketed into the immovable sides of the cast-iron stove with the noise of an attacking army.

"What—?" the hobo roared. He wheeled, seeking his enemy.

Drew darted back to the stove, seized a stick of firewood, and lunged. His swing struck the hand holding the razor; it skittered into a corner under the table.

The man screamed in rage and pain, struggled to grasp the shotgun with his broken hand. His eyes were terrible; they bored into Drew like those he had seen in cornered wild things. Unable to cock the shotgun, he flailed it desperately.

Drew sidestepped, whirled, and swung his club like a baseball bat with all the strength he could muster.

The blow connected; the shotgun clattered to the floor and caromed against the baseboard. The tramp fell to his knees in agony.

Drew swept his weapon over his head and hammered it across the man's head and shoulders. The effort brought him off his feet, and he staggered away against the back door.

The hobo sprawled, face down, on the floor. Drew stared, poised to renew his attack.

Mom swooped to his side. "Are you okay?" She laughed and cried and shook.

Afraid for a moment to trust his voice not to quiver, Drew nodded. "But he might come to any minute," he worried. "We gotta tie him up." He rummaged frantically around the kitchen, all the while praying his rubbery knees would hold him.

The bridle Dad had mended still hung on a hook behind the door. Drew yanked it down and dragged it to the form on the floor.

The man moaned, reached a hand to his head, and attempted to rise.

Drew scrambled astride the tramp's hips, wrenched back both arms, and encircled the wrists quickly with a length of rein from the bridle. He cinched it tight, then wrapped the trailing end securely around a leg of the cookstove.

The bum wavered on the edge of consciousness, trying to struggle.

Drew reversed his position quickly and sat facing the man's feet. He reached out with the other rein and snared both ankles. "There. All trussed up like the Thanksgiving turkey." He grinned shakily at Mom.

Something clanked on the floor. The gleam of metal protruding from the man's pocket caught Drew's eye.

"Granddad's watch! Mom, he stole Granddad's gold watch!" He swooped up the pocket watch and clenched it in his fist.

At the squeak of the screen door Drew whirled. Mom's hand flew to her mouth.

Poke sauntered across the porch, the lopsided grin lighting his face. "Well, little brother, no paying customers a'tall at the sale today. Your Moxie—"

The sight of Mom's face stopped him. Then he glimpsed the figure on the floor. "Hey, what—?"

Mom sobbed. "Oh, Arval, it was terrible! Where's Dad?" She looked behind Poke, to the truck in the yard and beyond.

"Down at the barn. What's going on here?"

Mom sagged; Poke shot out an arm and clasped her to him. She clutched him, weeping.

A roar came from the path. "Drew! Get down here this minute," Dad shouted. "What's the idea of leaving the milk sitting out in the barn?"

"Oh, Arval, tell him . . . tell him."

Drew shrugged. "It's okay, Mom, he doesn't know." He slipped through the screen door and met Dad on the path.

His father's face was dark. "Damn it, Drew, just when I think there's hope for you, you pull a stunt like this. I ought to whale you. . . . That milk may be pert near all that stands between us and starvation, and Millie going dry at that. You're old enough to know better than that."

Drew stared at his feet. "Dad, I—"

"None of your excuses, neither!" Dad lifted a hand as if to strike him.

"Walt!" Mom called from the porch. "Leave the boy be. You don't know...." She buried her face in Poke's shoulder, clutching his arms.

Dad's expression changed. He giant-stepped up the path, took the porch steps in one stride, and surveyed the scene in the kitchen. Then he gathered his wife into his arms. "My God, Poke. You went up against a man with a shotgun?"

"No, Dad! Not me—Drew! *Drew* did it, all by himself." He looked past Dad, to where Drew waited in the doorway. "Can't call you 'little brother' anymore. Took a man to do what you did."

Realization spilled over Dad's face. "Drew! My God, son, why didn't you tell me?" He handed Mom over to Poke, crossed to Drew, and grabbed his shoulders with both hands. "Are you all right, boy?"

Drew thought his knees would finally fail without the support of Dad's grip. He shrugged. "Yes, sir." He knew he should meet Dad's gaze, but his own eyes threatened to brim with tears.

His father made a choking sound and snatched Drew against his hard chest. Callused hands stroked Drew's head. "You might have been killed...."

His mother wiped her eyes. "If it hadn't been for Drew ... He was so grown up, so brave...." Her voice caught; she reached a shaky hand to Drew.

But still there were no words of praise from Dad.

Drew's voice returned. "He had Granddad's gold pocket watch!"

His father took the watch from Drew and looked at it

with a strange expression. "Wouldn't want to lose this, either."

Drew shook his head and retreated across the porch. "I'll see if I can save any of the milk." As he went out, he heard Dad cursing the tramp.

Snatches of Mom's explanation followed Drew down the path to the barn. ". . . anywhere, Walt . . . lost his job . . . his home . . . nowhere to turn for help . . . told me . . . on the road for over two years . . . cold, hungry . . . desperate . . . lost hope . . ."

Drew did not try to hear any more. It seemed to him that the most valuable thing any of them could lose was hope.

Then he heard an impatient bray. Moxie! Drew raced toward the barn and the waiting mule.

CHAPTER 9

The mule tossed his head and grunted a greeting, clearly pleased to be back with his new friend.

Drew hugged Moxie's neck and buried his head in the mule's stiff mane. He felt the animal's trembling cease under his hands.

After a glance up the path to be sure he was alone, he scooped an extra portion of feed for Moxie and forked a generous slice of hay bale into his trough.

When he grabbed a bucket to go to the well for water, Moxie stamped and tugged at his halter to follow.

"Take it easy," Drew said, laughing. "I'll be right back." He patted the mule's flank as he left.

While Moxie ate, Drew curried him carefully and brushed the dust and burrs from his tangled mane and tail. He talked softly as he worked. Moxie's ears flicked to show that he was listening, and his shrewd eyes reflected understanding.

Drew stayed with Moxie while Poke went to fetch the sheriff and until the lawman had come and gone with the tramp. By the time he remembered the milk, it had soured in the muggy heat that made it hard to imagine yesterday's cool spell.

The bark of Poke's coughing gave him away before he

reached the barn. Drew straightened and peered around Moxie's flank to the brightness of the doorway.

Poke waved the air around him to clear it of the dust stirred by his passing. "Hey, little br—buddy, Mom and Dad sent me to check on you. You've been out here so long we were getting worried. . . . I mean, after the tramp and all."

"Mom *and* Dad? Or just Mom?" Drew watched Moxie instead of his brother.

Poke eyed him. "Sure, Dad too. What's wrong? Are you okay, or what?"

"Nothing's wrong. It's just that . . . I'm all right."

"Dad said we should turn the hogs into the alfalfa."

Drew felt his eyes widen in surprise. "But Dad was mowing it." He remembered the towering cloud Dad had stirred as he tried to salvage even the short, withered crop mired in the dust.

Poke wiped his sweaty brow and resettled his hat. "Says it's too hard on Rose. She can't work that hard on so little to eat."

Drew nodded, recalling how the mare had tottered into the barn a few days ago. And how Dad, his eyes full of dust, or so he said, had squatted in her stall with tears streaming down his face.

With a shock Drew understood that his father had cried for his starving horse.

But stunted and doomed as it was, the failed alfalfa crop—if it could be cut and dried—would save the stock for a few more weeks. None of them, with the exception of the hogs, could eat green alfalfa.

He took a deep breath. "So Dad's just gonna write it off?"

Poke snorted. "What do you want him to do? Cut it

with a pair of scissors? Or maybe harness us to the mower?" He shook his head and sighed. "He says the hogs might as well make a good meal on it while they can and save the cornchop for the other stock. With another mouth to feed . . ."

Drew ignored the jab at Moxie and voiced his concern. "Think this means that Dad's given up?"

Poke endured a spasm of coughing and leaned against the mule's stall to rest. "Yeah. Well, I sure hope so."

Drew stared at the earthen floor. "You can go on back in. I'll see to the alfalfa." But not to turn the hogs into it, he added to himself.

"Hey, you sure you're okay?" Poke asked.

Drew nodded and avoided Poke's eyes. "You can take the milk as you go."

Poke frowned at the milk bucket. "Flies and dust and probably cat slobbers. But knowing Mom, she'll use it for butter and cheese." He hefted the solitary bucket. "Pretty soon we ain't even gonna have milk."

He glanced over his shoulder. "I forgot. Mom said to tell you we're going to Uncle Clay's for Saturday night supper, same as always."

Drew shrugged. Except for Poke not calling him 'little brother,' becoming a hero had changed nothing. He still could think of no way to save the farm or Moxie and the sheep and the rest of the stock.

Already the animals would have starved to death—or been shot—if not for the crib full of corn that Dad had not been able to sell because of the depression. It had seemed a tragedy at the time because of the family's own needs, but the unsalable corn had given their animals a reprieve. Now the crib stood nearly empty.

Drew scooped a measure of the severely rationed oats for bony Rose. He could not shake his guilt at failing to understand until now Dad's true concern for the stock.

Perhaps Dad's coldness was a front to hide his real feelings, Drew thought. Maybe his failure to say "well done" was something like that.

Clearly Drew had a lot of thinking to do. As an excuse for avoiding the rest of the family, he retrieved his rifle from the kitchen for cleaning and returned to the comfortable solitude and cool shade of the barn.

While he sat so quietly they thought he had gone, the rats, carriers of disease and despoilers of feed, crept out of hiding to glean the last bits from the mangers and stalls. Drew shot one for target practice.

"Drew!" Mom called from the kitchen after a while. "Ain't you going to Clayton's with us?"

Drew took careful aim, squeezed the trigger. The rifle report seemed louder in the barn. "Another rat bites the dust, a neat bullet hole right between the eyes," he announced to the shadows.

He raised his voice to carry to the house. "No, ma'am. I gotta stay here and worm the sheep." To avoid the lie, he scrambled up and doctored a flake of hay bale for Bo-Peep.

The screen door banged. Mom must figure he could make his own decisions now that he was a hero.

When the back door banged again, Drew glanced toward the house.

Mom and Dad and Poke trailed down the path. As she walked, Mom watched the covered bowl in her hands. She wore her coolest dress.

Drew remembered he had not eaten all day. Maybe he should go and get some of Aunt Martha's good fried chicken. But *somebody* had to worry about the family's terrible troubles.

While Poke went after the Oakland, Dad and Mom waited by the barn door. Drew went to hold Mom's dish while Dad helped her into the backseat of the car. When Dad went around to get behind the wheel, Drew slouched against the barn door to see them off.

Poke slid across the front seat and turned to his father. "I still wish you'd think it over, Dad," Drew heard him say. "About pressing charges against him, I mean. The poor old guy went off his rocker when the depression took everything he had. He couldn't help it. Putting him in jail wouldn't—"

Dad snorted and fished in his overall pockets for his car keys. "At least he would have three square meals a day in jail and wouldn't be breaking into people's houses and scaring them half to death."

Poke handed Dad his own set of keys. "He was desperate. Think how you'd feel if you was far from home and hungry and—"

"I have thought about it, son." Dad gripped the steering wheel with both hands. "I guess you're right. Since we got Granddad's watch back and no real harm was done, I won't press charges."

Poke grinned. "Thanks, Dad!"

The Oakland's old engine sputtered and backfired, but did not turn over. Drew heard Dad's curse, then Poke's soothing advice.

When the engine roared to life, Dad gunned it a few

times to demonstrate his mastery of the automobile. Then he released the brake and allowed the car to roll slowly down the lane.

Poor Dad, Drew thought. He would always be more at ease with a horse and wagon.

"Hey, Drew!" Jay jogged up the lane, seeming to appear out of the dust of the Oakland's leaving.

"Hey, Jay, come on in." To his surprise, Drew felt glad for the company. "Where's Billy Boy?"

"Aw, he decided it was too hot to go visiting." He pushed up his glasses. "Ever notice how dogs got more sense than people?"

Drew nodded. "Sure. Wish Dad would let me have a dog, but he says he can't afford another mouth to feed."

Jay settled beside Drew in the straw. "Shoot. We don't feed Billy much. He fends for himself—a rabbit here, a squirrel there." He watched Bo-Peep munching her tobacco-dusted hay, then jerked his head at Moxie. "Hey, I thought your dad was gonna sell your mule."

Drew shrugged. "So did he. But it turned out that no-body wanted him any more than Dad did." He smiled when Moxie flicked his big ears as if he knew they spoke of him. "I guess I'll get to keep him until we run out of feed. And then I reckon Dad will shoot the stock." His voice broke.

After a small silence, Jay cleared his throat. "Gee, buddy, you're a hero."

Drew shrugged. "News sure travels fast around here," he observed.

"Yeah, boy, it's probably all over the county by now," Jay agreed. "Sheriff stopped by our place to ask if we saw the tramp," he added importantly. "Weren't you scared?"

"Sure, I guess so."

"Kinda feel sorry for the ol' guy, though," Jay said thoughtfully. "Well, ain't you going to tell me about it?"

Drew found himself unwilling to think about the terrible morning, and his quick sketch of events for Jay's benefit left him feeling weak and trembly again. Some hero you are, he told himself.

At last Jay seemed satisfied and they sat in silence, with only the soft munching sounds from the animals to mar the peace.

After a while Jay said, "Sure does get lonely sometimes, don't it?"

Drew nodded. "I never do anything but work anymore, but I swear it don't do no good."

"Well, I had to get away from home for a little while. It's like a funeral over there. Everybody down in the dumps." He blinked and gazed curiously around the barn. "Hey, there's our old stilts!" He hauled the stilts out of a cob-webbed corner. "Remember these?"

"Sure. I remember when Granddad helped us make them."

Jay stepped up on the stilts and wobbled around the barn. "Gosh, how come we never play with these any-more?" He leaned the stilts back in their dark corner and squatted by Drew's side. "Remember those slingshots we made that summer?"

Drew grinned. "Yep. And I remember all the trouble we got into with 'em."

Jay stretched out in the straw. "And that paddleboat we sailed in the stock tank?"

"Oh, yeah. Wonder what ever happened to that thing?" Drew asked. "Kid stuff."

Jay sighed. "I don't know. Those were the good old days."

"Yeah. Corn was taller than Dad. And the wheat was yellow gold."

"I remember slices of ripe tomato as big as a saucer...." Jay said.

"And juicy, red, ice-cold watermelons we cadged from old man Engstrom."

Jay chose a stalk of straw for chewing and propped his head on a hand. "Drew, you know we might have to move?" He searched Drew's face.

"How come?" Drew tried to cover his dismay.

"Dad says our wheat's no good. Says if we can't raise a cash crop and a garden this summer we'll be licked. And he says if the drouth don't break we won't be able to do either." He rolled over onto his back. "And then we'd lose the farm and have to move."

A rat scurried across a stall opposite them. Drew whipped up his rifle and dropped the rodent in its tracks. He spoke soothingly to Bo-Peep and glanced at Moxie, who had not flinched at the loud report of the rifle.

"Hey, you're pretty good at that," Jay said.

Drew shrugged. "Just doing what I have to do." He settled back in the straw beside Jay. "Mom says us kids are having to grow up too quick, thanks to the depression."

Jay considered. "You are, I guess. I just mostly do what my dad tells me. I don't have responsibilities of my own like your sheep."

"Even Poke says I'm gettin' to be quite a man."

Jay snorted. "Aw, you just made that up."

"No, I didn't."

"Yes, you did." Jay shook his head in disbelief.

Drew stuck out a hand. "Here, look at my fingernails if you don't believe me."

Jay gaped. "What's your fingernails got to do with it?"

"Mom says if you tell a lie, it makes white flecks on your fingernails. You can see I ain't got no white specks." Drew flourished the hand.

Jay hooted. "Let me see the other one, Mr. Smarty-Pants."

Drew made a fist of the other hand.

"Oho! So you don't want me to see the other one, huh?" He lunged for Drew's hand.

They tussled in the straw until Drew remembered he had grown up. "Hey, I don't want to upset Bo-Peep. We better be quiet." He tried to regain his dignity.

Jay grinned. "Just 'cause I was getting the best of you. Next thing, you'll be telling me you're all set to be named Man of the Year!"

"Shoot!"

Jay shook his head in mock seriousness. "I don't know, Drew. Hilde's on the committee, you know." He winked. "I'd say you got a good chance."

"Come on, Jay. It ain't no popularity contest. They're serious about picking somebody who really deserves it."

"Fat chance. What could any of us kids at a dumb country school do to be Man of the Year?" Jay blinked. "Except you—saving your mom and all. No kidding, Drew. Nobody else has a chance now."

Drew shrugged. "Sure might make Dad—" He broke

off. If Dad was not proud of him now, he never would be, Man of the Year or not.

He watched Bo-Peep chew her tobacco wormer and reflected on the things that still separated him from manhood. "I guess about the only thing a man can do that I can't is chew tobacco."

"Shoot." Jay spat. "Ain't nothing to chewing tobacco."

"You tried it?" Drew knew Jay expected his surprise; he didn't disappoint him.

"Sure. When Dad could still afford tobacco," Jay said.

"Well, I'd try chewing if I . . . Come on." Drew scrambled up and took off at a run with Jay right behind him.

He had a vision of the tobacco tin resting on a shelf in the brooder house. Mom soaked it in water to worm her chickens, just as he used tobacco dust to worm the sheep.

It smelled as awful as the stuff men chewed, but what came out of the can in the brooder house was a kind of twisted stick.

"That ain't what Dad chews," Jay insisted.

"Let's try it anyway." Drew stuck a twist into the overall pocket meant for pencils. Jay followed suit.

On their way back to the barn, Jay stepped in a cow pie. He gagged and wiped his boot with some straw, then managed to soil his overalls with the straw.

"Whew!" Drew held his nose. "Good thing tonight's bath night."

"Heck," Jay said in disgust. "I'd have to take a bath now, even if it wasn't."

Drew laughed. "My mom says takin' too many baths can weaken you."

He settled into the straw near Moxie and measured how much of the tobacco twist to bite off. He leaned back against the side of a stall and chewed vigorously.

"This don't taste good," Jay complained.

Drew spat. "I sure don't like it." No wonder Bo-Peep ate so slowly, hungry as she was.

"I'll see you, Drew," Jay said, and hurried from the barn.

Drew stuffed the twist of tobacco back into his overalls and swallowed his queasiness. He looked up to wave good-bye to Jay and spotted Uncle Clayton's big Packard coming up the lane.

"What's the matter, nephew, can't handle your tobacco, huh?" Uncle Clayton's booming voice echoed in the barn.

Drew heard rustlings in the dark corners. "Hi. I thought everybody was over at your house."

"They are. I didn't like it 'cause you aren't." He squatted in the straw beside Drew. "Something wrong?"

Drew forced himself to meet Clayton's gaze. "Naw, I just felt like doing some thinking, that's all."

Clayton chewed a piece of straw. "Drew, I'm real proud of what you did today. That would be a piece of work for any grown man." He squeezed Drew's knee.

Drew grinned. "Thanks, Uncle Clayton."

"You really are the Man of the Year." Clayton's voice rumbled deep in his chest.

Drew groaned. "Not you, too. How'd you know about it?"

"Your dad and Poke told me a while ago. And they couldn't possibly give it to anyone else now."

Drew shrugged. "I don't know about that. It's just something those silly girls dreamed up, anyway." He watched dust motes float in the shaft of sunlight from the door. "I'd much rather hear it from Dad."

Clayton sat cross-legged in the straw. "Drew, your

father is very proud of you, too. It's just that he doesn't know how to show it. It's hard for some people. . . . But he is very proud of you."

"Did he tell you so?"

Clayton's gaze did not waver. "Not in so many words. But he doesn't have to. I know he's proud of you. And he loves you very much."

Drew shrugged. "Then why doesn't he ever say so?"

Clayton got to his feet, hitched up his overalls, settled his straw hat squarely on his head. "Tell you what, nephew, why don't you come home with me for some of Martha's fried chicken? Ain't no future in moping around here."

Drew shook his head. "If we're gonna be leaving here soon, I just figure I should soak it all up while I can."

Clayton cleared his throat and made a project of dusting the seat of his overalls. "Come on, then, walk me to the car." He headed for the door.

Drew followed. Beside the weathered gray barn stood their machinery, mutely rusting. There had been no money to run it, nor even to maintain it. Around the barn lot sagged neglected fences—it was a wonder they even held the tumbleweeds they hugged. Tired outbuildings leaned away from the wind and the chicken house clung desperately to its drooping roof.

When he reached the Packard, Clayton stopped and looked directly into Drew's eyes. "Don't be too hard on your folks, nephew. It breaks us parents' hearts to see our kids going through this." He swept an arm at the barnyard.

Drew took a deep breath. "Suppose you could see your way clear to lending us some money so's we wouldn't have to leave?"

Clayton leaned against his dusty car. "Drew, I hate to put more debt on your dad's shoulders to worry about. The last thing a man can lose is his pride." He inspected a patched tire on his Packard. "And you know, nephew, I'm not a rich man. I really can't afford to make a loan I know won't ever get paid back."

Drew nodded. "That's okay. I just hoped . . ."

Clayton opened the car door and lowered himself wearily into the driver's seat. The steering wheel seemed a toy in the grasp of his huge hands. "Tell you what I will do, though. I'll buy your sheep."

Drew blinked in surprise. "They ain't for sale."

"No? If your dad loses this place, they'll go at the foreclosure auction."

Drew stared at the ground.

"And he told me just now that the banker says either pay last year's interest on the note or get off the farm, by July first," Clayton added.

Drew looked up quickly, met his uncle's gaze.

"Think about my proposition." Clay's deep voice was earnest, man-to-man. "You're letting them slowly starve on that molasses-on-thistle mess you're feeding them. My way, you know they'd be taken care of right."

Drew's mind raced. "How much are they worth now?" The last market report he had seen had not held out much hope.

Clayton grinned. "Sheep's different from other livestock. Their wool's important, and some folks eat 'em. But I'd use yours to build up my flock. So, somewhere around seven dollars a hundredweight."

"But that would give Dad the money to leave on!" Drew's voice cracked.

"Or maybe pay the interest on the note, buy a little stock feed and groceries, and hang on here a few more months." Clayton started the Packard's engine, then looked back at Drew. "I should tell you that I just offered your dad the same deal."

"What did he say?"

"He said, 'The sheep belong to the boy,' and that he'd have to talk it over with you," Clayton replied.

"He still thinks I'm a boy," Drew said with a grimace.

Clayton chuckled. "I think what he means is that he thinks you're old enough to make the decision yourself, rather than for him to sell your sheep out from under you." He held Drew's gaze. "Look, I'm offering you a good deal here. When you get back on your feet you can buy them back, or I'll start you all over again like I did before. Where's your famous hope for the future?"

Drew shrugged. "Thanks for the offer, Uncle Clayton. I'll think about it. There's only one more week of school. Dad said he'd stay at least until school's out."

For days Drew thought of little else. Even the visit of the sheep shearer only served to remind him that nothing was the way it used to be.

Before the advent of these hard times, what was left of the wool money—after repaying Dad for pasture and feed—had been his. In those days he had been free to decide how it should be spent—perhaps for a new rifle, or overalls, or a ram.

But after this shearing, as had been the case last year in the absence of a cash crop, all the money would go toward the very survival of the family—whether on or off the farm.

CHAPTER **10**

"Come on, Jay, hurry up. We'll never live it down if we're late on the last day of school." Already several strides ahead of his friend, Drew quickened his steps.

"Well, is it my fault it's so danged hot? I hate to hurry when it's hot." Jay's usual good nature seemed as frayed as the collar of the starched shirt he tugged at. "Why couldn't our graduation be at night, like Poke's?"

By the time Drew trudged into the schoolyard, the bell was already ringing. No time to rest and cool off before going inside.

The stuffy schoolroom smelled of chalk dust and oiled wood. Drew rolled up the sleeves of his good white shirt and stuffed the tail once again into the waistband of the trousers Mom had insisted he wear for the last day of school.

He missed his comfortable overalls. It was too hot to dress up. Already a line was forming at the water bucket. He sighed. Spring had melted into summerlike weather, but still it had not rained.

After the Pledge of Allegiance and the singing of "America the Beautiful," Miss Jordan rapped on her desk with a ruler. "All right, eighth graders, why don't you clean out your desks while I discuss grades with the others. Your parents will be here in an hour for our graduation exercise." Her expression made it a command.

Drew heard a groan that could only be Jay's. He doubled over and peered under his desk top.

A sharp pain on the top of his head jerked him upright. A rubber band lay on the floor beside his desk.

He glanced around. All nearby heads bent to their tasks. He kept watch for a minute, then resumed pawing in his desk.

"Ouch!" A rubber band smacked him on the back of the neck and fell to the seat beside him. "All right, who's the wise guy?" he said aloud.

No one looked up, not even Miss Jordan.

But Drew no sooner returned to his task than another rubber band stung his shoulder and bounced onto his desk. He fingered it thoughtfully and studied the occupants of the seats within striking distance.

Hilde Simmons sat two seats away with the other seventh graders. He studied her profile.

She felt his gaze and glanced up, flushing prettily. In honor of the last day of school she wore a velvet ribbon in her hair and her Sunday-best dress.

He smiled. No, Hilde would not do that to him.

Although well within striking distance, goody-goody Richard Price would never do such a thing. Drew measured the others one by one and narrowed the field to two. It had to be either Jay or that Adams kid. Probably Jay. Adams would not have the nerve.

Drew waited until both Jay and Adams had their heads under their desk tops, then ducked quickly and closed his hand over the water gun he had spotted at the back of his desk.

He had forgotten about it. It had come attached to a package of Black Jack gum he had bought at the drugstore in town before all his money was gone. It just fit in his hand. Though it was only a pot-metal barrel attached to a rubber bulb, it would do the job.

But if he took the gun to the water bucket at the front of the room, someone would surely notice and tattle.

His gaze fell on the inkwell in the corner of his desk top. He glanced at Jay and Adams. Both were looking elsewhere.

Quickly he lifted the lid on his inkwell and eyed its contents. Cautiously he inched the hand concealing the gun to the top of his desk. If Adams or Jay looked his way, they must think he was merely toying with the inkwell. He pretended to look out the window and watched his progress out of the corner of his eye.

When the end of the gun barrel was submerged in the ink, he gently squeezed the rubber bulb in his palm. There was a soft sucking sound. He glanced around.

No one had looked up. Drew turned slightly in his seat, pulled a tablet from his desk, and leafed idly through it; but he studied Jay under lowered eyelids.

After only a few moments, Jay aimed a rubber band in Drew's direction and let it fly. The missile had not yet landed when Drew leaped to his feet.

Without a second's pause, he aimed the ink-filled water gun and squeezed the bulb.

The effect was all that he had hoped for. The ink spurted onto Jay's forehead and dribbled across his glasses. Drew whooped.

Jay swiped at his face with his hands and stared at their

inkiness. "Why, you . . . !" He sputtered and came after Drew.

Drew laughed and scurried down the center aisle, Jay on his heels. As they passed Miss Jordan at the front of the room, Drew glimpsed her startled face. He turned to confront Jay and danced backward along the wall, taunting his inky friend to catch him.

Miss Jordan leaped to her feet. "That's quite enough! Will you *little boys* kindly take your seats." It was not a question. "Honestly, Drew Ralston, aren't you ever going to grow up? I declare, you're a man one minute and a boy the next." She shook her head sadly.

Drew shrugged. Her words smarted as much as Jay's rubber bands.

But he noticed that Miss Jordan glanced frequently at the window. Then he saw that the day had darkened noticeably. And by the time the room had filled with parents and Miss Jordan had given out the perfect attendance and no-tardies awards, the daylight was copper colored.

"Well, folks, it looks like we'd best move our last-day-of-school picnic and eighth-grade graduation indoors." Miss Jordan smiled and gestured apologetically at the dust teasing against the window glass.

"All right, people." She gave her pupils a settle-down look. "We'll present the eighth-grade diplomas at this time."

She smiled at the graduates scrunched into the smaller desks in the front row. "When I call your name alphabetically, please come forward to receive your diploma." She stepped to her desk in the center of the dais where a small cardboard box held the rolled diplomas.

Hilde Simmons leaned to Miss Jordan's ear and whispered behind her hand.

Miss Jordan nodded and turned back to the assembly. She raised her voice so it would carry to the parents seated in the larger desks at the back of the room. "As many of you know, this year we will name a Man of the Year as a special social studies project. We, that is, the committee"—she smiled at Hilde, blushing behind the desk—"thought it appropriate to make the award to the recipient at the same time his diploma is presented."

Miss Jordan turned to her diploma box and picked up her roll.

Jay stretched beside Drew in the front row. Remnants of dried ink still stained his face. "What's a recipient, Drew?"

"I guess that's the winner." Drew yawned. He wished Miss Jordan would get on with it. She always dragged out the last day of school to the aching point. "You know, Jay, this is our last time in this old school."

Despite his eagerness to attend the high school in town, Drew felt a stab of regret. After eight years, he felt at home in the comfortable country school that Granddad had helped build.

"Yeah." Jay looked around the crowded room. "And I ain't sorry of it."

Miss Jordan cocked the first diploma. "Roy Adams," she announced.

Jay squirmed; he leaned to Drew and whispered, "I bet you're the receipt."

"Huh?" Drew glanced at his friend from the corner of his eye.

"The winner—the Man of the Year," Jay said.

Drew snorted. "You mean *recipient*."

Jay nodded. "Yeah."

Drew rolled his eyes. "Aw, I wish you'd quit harping on that."

"You'll see." Jay folded his arms on the small desk top and fixed his gaze on Miss Jordan.

"Peggy Evert." Miss Jordan smiled at Peggy as she stumbled onto the dais and, red faced, reached for her diploma with a trembling hand.

Jay snickered and drew a frown from the teacher. He slouched in his seat and leaned to Drew. "Can't be nobody but you. Nobody else has done anything to deserve it."

Drew sighed; Jay had not let go of it since he had saved Mom from the hobo. "Listen, Jay, for the last time—it was no big thing. Anybody else would have done the same."

"Yeah, but nobody else did. You did!" Jay pushed up his glasses.

Miss Jordan called, "Greg Gulick."

Drew risked a quick look at the dais and caught Hilde watching him. To his disgust, he felt a blush spread under his collar and up his face. He quickly looked away, but did not miss Hilde's self-conscious smile. He glanced at Jay.

"See! I told you," Jay chortled.

Drew shook his head and chopped his hand at Jay. "Sshh! Just because Hilde smiled at me don't mean anything."

"Jeremiah Justice," Miss Jordan sang, a little louder.

Jay shuffled across the dais. He turned to grin at his parents in the back of the room and fumbled his diploma. It rolled across the floor. When he bent to pick it up, his foot kicked it over the edge of the dais.

Someone on the front row scrambled to retrieve it and flourished it at Jay.

The audience laughed; the older boys hooted and clapped.

Jay turned crimson and hunched down in his seat.

"Congratulations, buddy," Drew said, laughing.

"Listen, Drew," Jay whispered urgently. "It's gotta be you. There's no one else left."

"Sure there is. There's Price or Smart or Tracy." He thought. "Or even Wilkins."

Jay scoffed, "Nope. You're it." He watched Miss Jordan expectantly.

"Richard Price." Miss Jordan beamed. Hilde Simmons handed her a ribbon-tied scroll. Drew saw the movement and groaned to himself.

"Ladies and gentlemen," Miss Jordan proclaimed. "District Seven's Man of the Year, Richard Price!"

As though from a great distance, Drew heard the applause of the parents and his classmates. He remembered to clap, then managed to turn a grin to Jay. "See, told ya."

Jay's face was angry. "Ain't right."

Miss Jordan pantomimed for quiet. "Ladies and gentlemen," she began. "Selection of our own Man of the Year turned out to be extremely difficult. So many candidates were deserving, a few outstanding."

Drew thought she looked his way.

"But when all the factors were weighed, including each individual's citizenship marks . . ."

Drew was sure she looked at him.

". . . the committee came to the conclusion that the award is, after all, for the man of the *year,* not the man of the *hour.*" More applause, scattered now.

That's about all the mileage she'll get out of that, Drew thought with satisfaction.

"Let's continue now with the presentation of the diplomas . . . Walter Drew Ralston . . ."

Drew got slowly to his feet and mounted the dais carefully. He was aware of applause, a smile from Hilde, and a loud whistle that could only be Poke's. Uncle Clayton's voice boomed over the rest.

"Speech!" Jay yelled.

Drew scowled and regained his seat gratefully.

The rest of the program blurred, even when Hilde recited the memory work she had practiced all year for extra credit.

"Excuse me, Miss Jordan," said a man's voice.

Everyone turned to see who had spoken up: it was Mr. Justice. "Maybe we better cut this short. Dust is getting worse." He jerked his head to the window. "I'd like to get home before my carburetor clogs up."

A titter rippled around the room, but there was a general chorus of agreement and nods from the rest of the adults.

The men brought in boards to bridge the row of desks along the side of the room, and the women spread white tablecloths over them. All the mothers set out their fried chicken, potato salads, pies, and rolls.

With the eighth-grade graduation over, Drew was through at the country school.

And now nothing held Dad on the farm.

CHAPTER **11**

When they left the school building, the sky hung low, heavy with dust. Barren trees clawed at the haze like the skeletons of marionettes. Tumbleweeds blew to the north and lodged against the fences in their path.

Drew knew that when the wind shifted, the dust and the tumbleweeds would blow back to the south.

"My law, I can't even walk against this wind." Mom held her handkerchief over her nose and mouth with one hand. The other anchored her old spring hat.

Poke helped her into the front seat of the Oakland.

Dad grunted. "Gravel even blows off the roads."

"Jay said their chicken house blew over," Drew offered, mainly to keep the conversation from turning to the lost Man of the Year award.

He held his breath while Dad turned the ignition key and kicked the starter hard. Remarkably, the engine coughed to life, and they joined the line of cars on the dust-choked road. The car was hot with the windows rolled up.

"If we had a lick of sense, we'd run like the devil," Poke said. "The only thing we've raised this spring is dust."

Drew screwed up his courage and worked hard to keep his voice deep and even. "If we can hang on, we'll still have the land when the rains come back."

"*If* they come back," Poke said scornfully.

"A body would think our luck would change sooner or later," Mom put in.

"It will rain again," Dad said. "It'll rain, and this country will bloom again."

Carefully, Drew asked, "Then how come you want to leave, Dad?"

"Son, I don't want to go. My father left me his land free and clear. He'd turn over in his grave if he knew I had mortgaged it. But what else could I do, crops failing year after year, market gone to hell?" He slowed before turning onto the highway and peered into the dust, more nuisance than full-blown dust storm this time.

Another car, as dirty as their own, dragged a chain on the concrete, spraying sparks, in an effort to dissipate the ever-present static electricity.

"My law, look there!" Mom pointed. Dust had banked up to the eaves of a house beside the road and around a tractor that had been left in the open.

"Yeah. You gonna farm in that?" Poke jerked his head.

Dad did not reply. He drove toward the gauzy horizon where gray land met gray sky. His hands gripped the steering wheel so tightly his knuckles whitened.

Drew cleared his throat. "Dad, if we sold the sheep to pay the interest, couldn't we stay?"

"Dang it, Drew . . ." Dad started. Then he softened. "Son, we got no garden, no money, and our stock is starving."

"Clayton says there's no work in the city," Mom said. "What would we live on there? At least here at home we got a roof over our heads. . . ."

Dad shook his head impatiently. "I know all that, Bea."

He steered the car onto their county road. "And I also know that the cistern is dry and the well at the stock tank is dry. That only leaves the well in the yard. If it goes dry . . ."

"Oh, Walt, knock on wood!"

Although Drew knew he was on dangerous ground, he persisted. "Couldn't we hang on a little longer if we sold the sheep and gave the money to the banker?"

The back of Dad's neck reddened. Drew caught sight of his angry face in the rearview mirror. "Listen, Drew, for the last time—you're only a boy. Even if we could save the farm, we have no crops and no garden. That means feed bills and grocery bills and . . ." He shook his head. "I know you're concerned. But you let me worry about things. When I decide what to do, I'll let you know."

"Yeah. Well, if you didn't have me like a stone around your neck, you'd have a better chance," Poke put in. "I'm just a burden to you. I can't get work. I got no future here. You'd all be better off. . . . You might be able to hang on here, if that's what you want, if I just hit the road."

Mom gasped. "Arval, no! Both of you. Just hang on a little longer. I know we can." When she tugged at her hat, her fingers were crossed.

After a moment, Poke said, "Well, without me you'd have one less mouth to feed in the meantime."

The Oakland labored to breathe the dusty air as Dad shifted down to turn into their lane.

Then he gunned the engine abruptly, and the car jounced past their gate. "Let's go on into town. I'll talk to the banker one more time. Maybe . . ." The word seemed to echo inside the closed car.

Drew thought about his sheep. If losing them meant

saving the farm . . . He stared out his grimy window.

A gas pipeline snaked across a field, bare and exposed. Drew remembered when the pipelines had been laid. They'd been buried at least two feet deep.

Huge rocks stood in the fields along their route like monuments. Once they had been so deep in the ground that the strongest plowshare never touched them.

He saw the grain elevator in the distance, rising majestically out of the plains, towering like the battlements of a medieval castle. When he was in second grade, it had reminded him of a fairy tale Miss Jordan had read aloud. Now he closed his eyes to shut out the ugliness.

Back then the rains had come on time and the wheat fields seemed to go on forever. Horizon to horizon they waved, the grain thick and heavy. The world was all blue and gold: electric blue sky, butter yellow sunshine, and amber wheat. The fresh wind smelled of new-mown hay. People smiled and waved, and the cattle were fat and sleek.

He and Poke had ridden with Dad to take a load of their wheat to the elevator.

He had stood at the foot of the grain-elevator castle and whispered, "Rapunzel, Rapunzel, let down your golden hair!"

And when he looked up, the golden grain had cascaded down in a torrent that shimmered and shone in the sunlight and seemed alive, filling all the bins with the rich harvest.

When he felt the car jolt over the railroad embankment at the edge of town, Drew opened his eyes. The battlements of the grain elevator still loomed over the tracks, but the only thing moving around it today was the dust drifting against its side and between the railroad ties.

Dad parked the Oakland in front of the bank. "Looks like they're busy. You all find something to do. Meet me back here after a while." He got out and hitched up his overalls. He had worn a suit to Poke's graduation at the high school, Drew remembered.

Mom sniffed. "Oh, law. Don't know what good it is to get to town with no money to spend."

Drew almost laughed. But he knew Mom was happy for the chance to visit the dry goods store. She would finger the yard goods and shiny new buttons, then go to the dime store next door.

She would look at fancy dishes and costume jewelry, but she would buy nothing. If she had any money, she would buy tennis shoes or overalls for him before buying anything for herself.

But if Dad was patient, she would go on to the drugstore and leaf through the magazines, lingering over pictures of the latest fashions, the new styles in curtains and furniture. Then she would suddenly feel self-conscious in her best, long-out-of-style, faded dress and hurry back to the car.

She shouldn't care so much, Drew thought. The last time he was in town, he'd seen ladies in dresses made of feed or flour sacks.

As he and Poke sauntered down the street, Drew recalled how he used to feel in a holiday mood on their infrequent visits to town.

Even now Poke whistled as they walked. "I'll tell you for sure I'd a lot rather live in town."

Drew shook his head. "Not me, boy."

"Yeah. Well, you're just like Dad and Granddad. Me, I hate that danged farm."

Drew considered. That explained a lot of things about Poke. "How come you never told me that before?"

Poke grinned and clapped him on the shoulder. "Well, you're getting all grown up now, buddy. I can talk to you."

Drew squared his shoulders and matched Poke's stride. He saw that the cracks between the bricks in the street were filled with dust, and dirt drifted along the curb and piled high in doorways.

All along Main Street storekeepers busily swept the sidewalks. At Monkey's, the manager was sweeping, although the front window had been boarded up.

"What happened?" Poke asked the sweeper.

"Wind. Blew some gravel right through it!" He shook his head as if he still couldn't believe it. With each push of the broom, some dust blew away and some settled again to the sidewalk.

"You're fighting a losing battle," Drew said.

The merchant nodded sadly. "Aren't we all!"

A dirty car slowed as it passed them. Drew recognized several of Poke's former classmates.

"Hey, Ralston," a youth yelled from the car window, "how's your crazy mom?"

Drew felt Poke tense beside him. His own face burned hot, and hateful words welled in his throat.

But Poke only grinned. "Ain't it a shame that some people ain't mature enough to know that everybody has his own way of coping with trouble."

The youths laughed, and the car sped away.

Some things in town had not changed: posters still leaned in the window of the drugstore. One was printed in bold black blocks. "Join Our Prayer Band," it read. "Join Us and Help Us Pray for Rain."

Poke pointed. "I like this one better."

The second poster had been crudely lettered on bright orange paper. "Root Beer Drinking Contest! All the Root Beer You Can Drink for 5 Cents!"

Drew's mouth watered. For a long time there had been no money for soda pop.

"I can win that contest easy," Poke declared.

Drew eyed him. "Can we spend a dime?"

Poke counted the change in his pocket. "Yeah. Just." He slapped Drew on the back. "We gotta celebrate our graduations, little br—er, buddy."

Inside the door Poke paused to glance at the new stock of western magazines. He recounted his money, gave a nickel to Drew, and then turned away from the magazine rack with a sigh.

At the soda fountain, an elderly soda jerk with a sunburned bald head handed them each a frosty mug of ice-cold root beer and collected their coins.

Drew thought the icy root beer smelled as good as it tasted. The foam tickled his nose and gave him a sudsy moustache. When he had downed the root beer, he slid the cool mug over his forehead.

He inspected himself in the long mirror behind the fountain. The hot sun had browned his skin; he looked like an Indian. A curly-haired Indian.

He grinned at Poke's reflection in the mirror. "Poke, what did you mean a while ago when you said I'm just like Dad?"

Poke wiped the root beer foam from his lips. "Just what I said. You think alike and you feel alike. Why do you think they named you after him? He saw you lying there in that bassinet and knew you were a son after his own heart."

Drew shrugged. Clearly that was something to think about.

Overhead the slowly rotating ceiling fan only stirred the stale, medicine-smelling air. The soda fountain, once an oasis on stifling Kansas afternoons, was deserted. The wind blowing through the open door across the sun-soaked bricks and concrete seemed out of an oven.

Drew spun on his stool and looked around. Dingy sheets and canvas tarpaulins covered all the merchandise on the counters. If he had the money to buy anything new, he would have to wash it before he could use it. Even all the pharmacist's jars and bottles were dust-covered and gritty.

The druggist himself tiredly pushed a muddy mop across the once-white tiles on the floor.

"Poke." Drew pivoted on the stool and once again sought his brother's eyes in the mirror behind the fountain. "Then how come Dad likes you better than me?"

"Ahhh." Poke banged his empty mug on the counter. He tossed his sandy hair back from his forehead and swiped at the sweat and freckles on his face. "Fill 'em up," he ordered.

He turned on his stool and looked at Drew. "Dad doesn't like me better, buddy," he said slowly. "He just doesn't expect as much from me as he does you."

"Huh?"

Poke grinned. "Well, you think about it. You'll understand what I mean when you get a little older."

Drew sipped his second root beer. It went down as easily as the first. "Poke, you ain't really gonna leave, are you?"

Poke pushed his hat to the back of his head and met

Drew's gaze directly. "Yeah. Can't say when for sure, but as soon as I get up the nerve, I'm gone."

"But why? What good will that do?"

"Look . . ." Poke coughed. "Maybe you're not old enough to understand now, but someday you will."

Drew sighed. He wished he knew when to expect that magic day when he would be old enough to understand all of life's mysteries.

His third root beer took longer to drink. He had more time to think about Poke's leaving. "Poke, it's not your fault the depression came. You gotta stay home with us."

Poke clumped his mug down with a flourish. "Dad will never leave, Drew. And I've *got* to." He nodded to the mug. "Again!"

Drew decided to call it quits.

The sunburned soda jerk gave Poke a questioning look with the fourth mugful. "Average is about three," he said. "Four's the record so far."

"I can't lose," Poke declared as he hefted the brimming mug.

Drew cleared his throat to keep his voice from cracking. "Poke, how come you're running away?"

"Running away?" Poke repeated. "You think I'm running away?" He shook his head. "Listen, Drew, this little trip I'm planning takes all the guts I can muster. I'd much rather stay home with you and face the dusters and the hungry hoboes and shooting stock and slowly starving on a skinny-rabbit-and-canned-tomato diet."

"Then stay!"

Poke bought time by gulping his root beer. "I wish it was that easy," he said softly. "I'm old enough I should be out on my own, and not hanging around being a burden to Mom and Dad. It'll be just one less mouth to feed, little buddy."

Drew traced the wet outline of the mug before him on the shining counter. "Where you heading?"

Poke wiped the foam from his mouth and considered. "The train to Kansas City, I guess. I ain't hankering to pick cotton in Arizona or grapes in California. I'll try for a job in the city. If all else fails, I guess I'll ride the rails."

Drew watched his brother's face in the mirror. "How can you even think about becoming a hobo after what happened . . . in the kitchen?"

Poke sipped his root beer and said nothing.

It seemed unreal to Drew, sitting here in the drugstore calmly discussing Poke's uncertain future over root beers, as if they were talking of what colt he would break for the 4-H fair—or what college he would attend.

"It's dangerous, Poke, hopping trains," he said softly.

Poke tilted back his head to drain his mug. "Yeah. Well, I don't plan to get real fancy until I learn the ropes. I'm just gonna sneak on while she's stopped for water or coal, to begin with."

"You're tied for first," the soda jerk said respectfully when Poke brandished his empty glass.

Poke grinned. "Well, I said I could do it and I will. Fill 'er up!"

But Drew saw the shadow of a doubt pass over Poke's face.

"You gotta drink it in five minutes to be legal," the soda jerk warned as he set down the fifth mugful. It brimmed over onto the counter.

"Poke, you'll bust," Drew protested.

"Nope. I can do it." He took a sip. Then another. Then he leaned his head back and tilted the full mug to his face.

He eyed the Roman numerals on the fancy clock hanging over the fountain. He seemed to time his swallows as the clock ticked off the seconds. His Adam's apple bobbed in perfect rhythm to the big hand's march toward the five-minute mark.

At the very last second, Poke banged down the mug. Only a little foam lingered on its bottom. "Five!" he gloated, but he swallowed hard.

"Well, I'll be!" The soda jerk gave a low whistle. "Four minutes and fifty-nine seconds! Didn't think you could do it."

Poke's freckles had never been clearer in his pale face. "Well, what do I win?"

The druggist strolled over to the soda fountain. "Why, the title," he exclaimed, and laughed. "And another glass of root beer!" He peered over his spectacles and grinned at Poke.

Even Poke's freckles seemed to pale. "Great. But can I have a rain check?"

The druggist's smile faded. "Rain? What's that?" Then, "Sure, son. Come in any time." He clapped Poke on the shoulder and turned back to his mop bucket.

"Yeah. Well, if I'm still around, I'll do that." Poke led the way onto the gritty sidewalk. Since there was no water to spare for washing cars, the curbs were lined with vehicles heavy with layers of encrusted dust.

Poke lifted his hat and swiped a finger across his brow, then fanned his flushed face with the hat. He sought Drew's eyes. "Listen, buddy, you gotta promise me you won't tell Mom and Dad about our talk or where I'm going!"

Drew shrugged. Mom was unhappy enough just *thinking* of Poke leaving.

Poke grabbed Drew's overall straps. "Promise me!" His green eyes were relentless.

Maybe Dad could convince him to stay, Drew thought.

Poke shook him. "Promise me!"

"Okay, okay! I promise." But he was sorry immediately and trailed after Poke in despair.

Mom and Dad were waiting at the car. Mom sat in the backseat. Her face unreadable, she faced the front in silence.

Their father stood outside. "You drive, Poke," Dad said. He got in front without another word.

"What did the banker say, Dad?" Drew asked.

"I said when I decide what to do, I'll let you know," Mr. Ralston snapped. But after a moment he flicked a glance at Drew over his shoulder. "Son, the banker said some new mortgage protection law—a moratorium, they call it—is making it harder for banks to foreclose on some farmers, but he'll have to see if it applies to me. Us."

Drew nodded and tried to keep the elation from his face. Granddad always said not to confuse one battle with the whole war.

Dad cleared his throat. "But like I said, even if we could save the farm, we've still got to have some kind of income to live on. The banker says he definitely can't loan me any more. I just paid up the filling station and the grocer with the last of the wool money."

Drew leaned his head back against the dusty car seat.

Uncle Clayton was right. Losing the sheep was not the worst thing that could happen. Leaving the farm was.

But if he agreed to sell Clayton the sheep, how could he be sure Dad would not use the money to leave? Now did not seem to be a good time to ask.

Poke cruised through the residential section of town, as dirty and ugly as the countryside. Up and down the brick streets the townspeople also fought the dust.

Housewives swept porches where several inches of dust had accumulated overnight. In backyards boys beat at rugs stretched over clotheslines; dust billowed around them.

Dad grunted. "Gas is twelve cents a gallon, Poke. Can't afford no joyriding."

Drew welcomed the road for home, but found it difficult to keep his bearings. Dust dunes now rose where once had waved a sea of wheat.

Something dark against a dune caught his eye. He focused on it. Corpses. Dead cattle. Huddled together, they had dropped where they stood, suffocated by caked dust in their nostrils.

He looked quickly away. Dust scudded across the pavement and collected on the low side of curves. He had heard that sometimes the dunes blocked the roads completely.

Dad read an old newspaper he had picked up at the bank. "Listen to this," he hooted. "Says, 'If God can't make it rain on Kansas, how can the New Dealers hope to succeed?'" He chuckled without humor.

The "New Dealers," Drew knew, were what newspaper people called the men in charge of running President Roosevelt's "New Deal" for the down-and-out farmers—

programs not popular with everyone. Even though Dad liked President Roosevelt, he often complained that the New Deal helped only the big land owners and corporate farms, not the small, independent farmers like him.

"I say we ought to get out of here while we still can," Poke said. "We could make it to Kansas City on the sheep money." He darted a glance at Drew in the rearview mirror.

Drew held his breath, but Dad refused the bait.

Poke tried again. "I saw Henry Justice in town after school the other day. He'd been all over trying to borrow money. Says he's licked."

Drew thought his heart had stopped.

Dad glanced at Poke around the edge of the paper.

"That moratorium law couldn't help him. They're pulling out," Poke added, his voice husky.

Drew groaned aloud and bit his lip to quell the anguish.

Dad folded the paper carefully. "Well, I'd say things are looking up," he said with irony. "It says here that the wheat allotment is finally filtering down to us. We can apply for it any time now."

"Well, that's what I call a 'New Deal' for sure," Poke said with a grin. "The technocrats will pay us cash money for not growing wheat that we can't grow anyway!"

CHAPTER **12**

By the time the car approached the turnoff to the Justice farm, Drew felt the need for activity.

He scooted forward and leaned against the dusty back of the front seat. "Dad, reckon you could drop me off at Jay's road? I ain't been over there in a coon's age, and if you don't need me this afternoon . . ."

"All right." Dad leaned his head against the car seat, and Poke braked in the road.

Drew clambered out of the car and looked back over his shoulder. Dad should be mad and stubborn and strong, he thought. Not tired and beat. Not ready to give up. He had scarcely been out of the house for days, strange behavior for a farmer.

Dad had not even asked whether he had turned the hogs into the alfalfa, Drew remembered. He hurried away from the road to escape the dust of their leaving.

A few dingy clouds floated overhead as he walked down the dusty road. He wondered if they could be mirages, like the lakes that suddenly appeared before them in the highway. But the clouds were casting shadows. The shadows slid over the road, the crisped weeds, the restless tumbleweeds.

"Mirages don't cast shadows, do they?" he asked aloud.

He tilted his head back and shouted, "Come on, clouds! Make some rain!"

He felt better then, and pushed aside his worries about the sheep, about the future, about leaving the farm. He would not even allow thoughts of Poke's confirmation that soon the Justices would be moving. Although it was too hot to run, he broke into an easy jog to keep from thinking.

After all, school was out. The whole summer stretched before him. Maybe Jay wouldn't be leaving right away. Drew struggled to find his usual beginning-of-summer thrill as he turned into Jay's lane. He was unprepared for what he saw as he rounded the bend to the house.

The Justices' ancient Hupmobile was parked across the front steps to the house. Most of the family's possessions appeared to be piled on the dusty car. Drew had seen caravans of such cars on the highway—always old, always impossibly laden. And always peopled with dust-beaten farm folks with haunted eyes and ragged, skinny kids.

Drew stared, an empty feeling in the pit of his stomach. Homemade barn-board racks clung to the car, along the back fenders and across the roof at right angles to the running boards. The boards were loaded with the stuff of poor-farm householding: mismatched dishes, lumpy mattresses, a washboard, a chipped dishpan.

Two many-patched tires were tied securely along one side of the car; behind them were wedged gunny sacks bulging with unironed clothes and holey shoes. Atop the car a cardboard box of dented pots and pans rested on a washtub turned upside down over a suitcase tied shut with binder twine.

Beside the box on the roof were more rope-tied boxes

and bags of clothing and blankets. A single chair's wooden legs stuck crazily out of the heap. A faded five-gallon gasoline can perched on one rusty fender.

Jay's father circled the car, lashing everything down with a rope that webbed the whole automobile, around door handles, headlights, running boards, fenders, up and over the roof, around washtub and boxes and bags.

Only one door remained untied. Drew guessed it to be both entrance and exit.

He wrenched his gaze away from the car. Propped open with a rock, the screen door gaped on the empty house like a toothless mouth.

Looking like a scared little girl in her print dress and bobbed hair, Jay's mother stood on the porch and stared at the dead farm. Drew wanted desperately to speak to her but could think of nothing to say.

Jay's younger brother and sister wandered out of the house. The little girl clutched a rag doll to her breast; tears slid down dirty rivulets on her cheeks.

The boy gripped a baseball bat and a tattered glove. The child's eyes sunk into his face like black holes.

Mr. Justice's glance flickered over the children. "I said *one* toy apiece."

The little boy swallowed. "It is just one, Daddy. What good's a bat without a glove, or the other way around?"

Justice started to argue, thought better of it.

The boy stowed his treasures in the backseat of the Hupmobile.

Jay's little sister stood uncertainly on the porch, clinging to her mother's dress and watching Drew intently. She had no shy smile for him today.

Mr. Justice turned to Drew at last. He jerked his head. "Jay's down to the barn."

Drew plodded to the barn. When he stepped into the shadowed coolness of the barn from the hot brightness, he could not see Jay. He swiped at the sweat stinging his eyes and glanced around.

"Here I am." Jay's voice came from the shadows.

Drew approached the sound. He peered into the gloom and could just make out Jay kneeling beside his dog in an empty stall. Even in the dimness, he could see tears welling in Jay's eyes.

Through a crack in the boards, a shaft of sunlight glinted on the blued barrel of Jay's old rifle.

Awful realization swept over Drew. He fell to his knees beside Jay. "Oh, Jay," he whispered. One hand gripped his friend's shoulder; the other reached shakily to the dog.

Jay wiped his nose on his sleeve and drew a deep, shaky breath. "Dad says I can't take Billy Boy. . . . I can't just leave him to starve. I've got to shoot him." His voice broke, and he sank his chin upon his chest.

Drew gazed at Billy Boy, mostly to avoid watching the suffering of his friend. The dog regarded them both with liquid brown eyes; understanding seemed to dwell in them.

Drew wished he could vanish, or turn off his mind.

At last Jay rose. In slow motion he lifted the rifle to his shoulder. Billy looked up at him unflinchingly.

Drew's eyes brimmed. "Wait!" he cried, and leaped to his feet.

Jay seemed to welcome the reprieve, however brief, and lowered the gun. He turned to Drew woodenly.

"Wait," Drew repeated and held up a shaking hand. "I'll

take him," he blurted. "He can come and be my dog." After the way Dad had carried on over Moxie, it probably meant only a delay in execution, he thought, but Jay did not have to know that.

Jay's face lightened a shade. "What about your dad?" He pushed up his glasses with a trembling hand.

Drew shrugged. "Once I get Billy home, what can he say?" He reached down and patted Billy's head. The dog regarded him soulfully.

"Look, Jay, at least this way you don't have to shoot him, and you can rest easy knowing I've got him." To his surprise, his words sounded calm and soothing.

"Yeah, sure," Jay breathed in relief. "Billy likes you, and he'll make you a good sheep dog. . . ." His voice threatened to break again. "And when we get settled, I'll write you, and you can let me know how he's getting along—"

"Jay!" Mr. Justice called hoarsely.

Now that the crisis of Billy Boy was settled, the larger one of the loaded car and vacant house loomed. "Where you going?" Drew asked softly.

"Dunno. West." Jay brushed the straw from his overalls. "Dad says we lost the place." He scanned the empty barn. "Took all the stock, machinery, everything. Left us just our clothes and stuff. Gotta move. . . . Nothing to live on here, anyway. Let me finish the eighth grade. Dad says that's probably all the schooling I'll get."

"Gosh, Jay . . ." Drew put a hand on his friend's shoulder.

Jay met his gaze. Drew saw that Jay felt the same grief, too large for speech.

Jay turned in the circle of Drew's arm and clasped him

fiercely. Then he stepped back, caressed Billy Boy's head, shouldered his rifle, and ran from the barn.

The dog started to follow, but Drew called to him to stay.

Billy obeyed, but he whined softly after Jay. His ears perked at the few words the Justices exchanged at the car.

Though Drew did not want to watch their departure, he moved to the door. He did not want to watch that family pile into their ancient car, their poor belongings tied on around them. He tried to look away, but he had to see the old car bump slowly down the dusty lane and over the railroad tracks for the last time.

He could not look away when Jay turned and waved a hand, managing a brave grin.

Drew stood there long after the car had disappeared under a pillar of dust. The hot wind sighed through the hollow house, the deserted barn. He looked around him at the sagging fences, the dilapidated sheds, the sun-cooked, wind-ravaged, dust-buried farm. Tumbleweeds blew across the porch of the derelict house and lodged in the open door.

He clenched a fist and struck it hard against the side of the abandoned barn. *That* to the depression and the drought!

After a moment he snapped his fingers to Billy Boy and trailed down the lane to the road. His tail between his legs, Billy looked back over his shoulder. He hesitated.

Drew turned, whistled, and called to the dog. Billy Boy followed him down the lane.

Walking slowly and stopping often to rest and think, Drew imagined the look on Dad's face when he saw the dog. "I can't afford another mouth to feed," he would say.

But even if Dad ordered the dog shot, Drew decided, it would be better than letting Jay shoot him.

By the time he trudged up the path to home, the sun had begun to sink in dust-reflected glory. No doubt Dad and Poke were at the barn, having to do his chores as well as their own.

Let them; he would take his medicine. He heard Mom in the kitchen, humming "Happy Days Are Here Again." He thought he detected a mournful note in the happy song, but it seemed strangely comforting.

He stationed Billy Boy on the screened-in porch and stepped into the ovenlike kitchen.

Her face flushed and shiny, his mother looked up from her worktable and flashed the smile that seemed reserved for him alone. "You're late," she said sternly.

He stood before her. "Yes, ma'am," he replied meekly.

She smiled again and ruffled his hair. "We thought maybe you'd been stolen by the gypsies or sailed down the crick to the ocean," she teased, referring to half-forgotten childhood escapades.

"No, ma'am." His voice was thick with the pain of the afternoon.

She heard it. "What's wrong?" She wiped her hands on her apron and smoothed back his hair, looked deep into his eyes.

He told her. The story poured out like butter on warm cornbread, but he didn't cry.

Dad and Poke came in quietly while he told of the relinquished home, the unhappy children. Dad squatted on the porch to speak to Billy Boy.

"Good-looking dog, son," Dad said. "Smart eyes." He sighed deeply. "Poor Justice." Wearily he hung his hat on its hook and ladled water into the washbasin. Almost to himself he added, "We'll cross that bridge when we come to it."

Poke sank into a chair, his face white and pained. "Well, I can only believe they'll be better off in the long run." He glanced at Drew. "I fed and watered Moxie and the sheep for you, buddy."

Drew nodded. "Thanks." He ushered Billy Boy into the kitchen. The dog must feel awkward and uncertain in his new home, he thought.

His room under the eaves was stifling, but for once Drew was scarcely aware of it. Billy Boy sniffed out a place near the window and plopped down with a sigh.

Drew's eighth-grade diploma waited on his bed. As he looked at it, he felt a strange nostalgia. The scroll seemed to belong with the rest of his childhood souvenirs.

He withdrew a cracker tin from its hiding place under the far corner of his feather tick mattress. He lifted the tiny latch and dumped the contents of the box onto the comforter. Granddad's silver pocketknife gleamed softly in the rosy sunset. He caressed it with his fingertips.

He smiled to himself at Granddad's handmade cross from the grave of some forgotten pet they had buried in a cigar box. There was a tarnished bell from an old canary cage, and a polished pebble from the creek—the one he had thought so beautiful he could not bear to part with it. He shook his head sadly and rolled it on his palm. The sandblasted buffalo vertebrae he had found in the sand hill always conjured up images of the pioneers' Kansas more clearly than any history book.

Drew added the diploma to the cache and repacked the little tin box, so bright and beautiful in its own right. Then he lifted the mattress and replaced the box in its hiding place. His pillow smelled of dust. He slapped the comforter; dust wafted into the air.

Billy Boy lifted his ears and cocked his head.

Drew spoke to him reassuringly and joined him at the window high above the farm. Together they watched the twilight creeping over the plains. "I wonder where Jay is going to sleep tonight," he said to Billy Boy.

A breath of cooler air lifted Drew's hair. He looked down upon dust-scoured buildings and tired fences and hungry animals that uneasily reminded him of the Madsen and Justice farms. But he soaked up the sights and the sounds of the farm at evening and cherished them.

He was sure now. He could sacrifice the sheep to save the farm.

But again the question came to haunt him. What if Dad insisted on using the money to leave, rather than to stay?

Like Billy Boy, he would have to live one day at a time.

CHAPTER **13**

Drew heard his mother's light step in the stairwell behind him. He worked to pull his long face into shape.

Billy Boy's tail thumped on the floor when Mom's head appeared in the doorway. She fanned the air in front of her as she pushed into his room. "My law, I don't see how you breathe up here."

Then she gasped. "How many times have I told you it's bad luck to hang a hat on a doorknob?" She grabbed Drew's baseball cap off the doorknob and flung it across the room. It landed right side up on his bed.

Drew snorted. "How many times have you told me it's bad luck to put a hat on a bed?"

"Oh, law, what have I done?" She sprang to the bed, snatched the hat, and dropped it on the floor as if it were alive. With crossed fingers she passed a hand over her eyes, seeming to search her memory for a charm that could undo the spell.

After a moment she perched on the edge of his bed and patted the comforter beside her. Dutifully Drew went to sit next to her.

Billy Boy got up stiffly and stretched. He sniffed at the hat, then resettled himself at Drew's feet.

"Dad and Poke can use some help shelling popcorn for

supper," Mom said. "We want to celebrate your and Poke's graduations."

Though Drew saw little reason to celebrate, he swallowed the retort forming in his mind. Mom meant no harm.

"Do I have to?" He avoided looking at her.

"Honey, the whole idea is to take our minds off our troubles. It won't work if you're sulking up here." She pushed back the curls from his sweaty brow. "I'm sorry you didn't win that award. We all think you really deserved it."

He turned to look at her. "You think that's why I want to be alone? Because I didn't win the Man of the Year award?"

She sniffed but made no reply.

"Well, it isn't." His voice cracked and it came out like a growl.

His mother patted his thigh and smiled tightly. "I know. But it should be. I know how painful it is to grow up. Especially in these times."

She stood up. "But I would like for you to come be with the rest of us downstairs. We haven't had any popcorn for a long time. Maybe it'll help us remember what good times we used to have. Besides, I can't keep the apples any longer."

She tickled his chest and forced a grin from him. "So we'll have popcorn and apples and cold milk for supper just like we used to every Friday night. Doesn't that sound good?"

Drew nodded and his mouth watered. Like everything else, the supply of popcorn had fallen dangerously low and had been rationed. What was once routine was now truly cause enough for celebration.

"Just whose idea was this little celebration?" He picked at the tufts of yarn on the comforter without looking at her.

She turned back to the bed. "Mine. Why?"

He shrugged. "I just thought . . . Does it seem to you like Dad's given up? Like maybe he don't even care anymore?" He searched her face for her true answer while she considered how to reply.

She sank back to her seat beside him. When his gaze flickered away, she cupped his chin with a tiny hand and turned his face toward her. She studied it wordlessly.

"I mean, he hardly even *looks* at the farm anymore," Drew blurted. "He never did ask if I turned the hogs in on the alfalfa, and half the time he don't even write in his daybook anymore."

She patted his cheek and sighed. "So you do see why the popcorn is so important. Will you help me cheer Dad up?"

He snatched his cap off the floor and burst through the door and down the steps two at a time. Nothing was more important than keeping Dad on the farm. He heard Billy Boy's claws clicking on the stairs behind him.

Dad and Poke were already busy at Granddad's old house. Drew fumbled with the door in the near darkness and stumbled into the lantern light inside. Billy slipped in beside him.

Drew blinked his eyes at the light. The others had drawn their makeshift seats around the steel popcorn barrel, a make-do Dad had picked up at the bakery in town to keep the rats out of the popcorn.

Since the miniature ears of popcorn were too small to feed through the regular corn sheller, the tedious and time-consuming job must be done by hand. But it allowed a wonderful, quiet time to gossip, to plan future farm operations, and to have serious discussions.

Already Dad and Poke had a pile of shelled corn in the blue graniteware kettle on the floor between them. Drew pulled his own upended pail into the circle of lantern light. He adjusted the gunnysack cushion and sat down carefully.

Across from him his grandfather's old five-gallon galvanized bucket still waited, its empty presence almost like a fourth person in Granddad's former living room.

Like still another ghostly presence, rat tracks trailed through the dust to a darkened corner, where ominous rustlings reminded Drew of their reality.

Billy Boy went to greet Poke, then rested his head on Dad's knee. His tail waved.

Drew snapped his fingers. "Here, Billy."

"It's all right, son." His father stroked the dog's head. "Good dog, Billy." He sighed. "Poor Justice. Having to leave everything he's worked for . . ."

Poke coughed. Before he could repeat his claim that the Justice family would be better off, Drew said, "I'll bet Jay's scared. They didn't even know where they were going. I wonder where they'll sleep tonight."

At mention of Jay's name, Billy Boy's ears lifted. With a sigh he settled to the rough planking at Drew's feet.

Drew felt Poke's stare, probably to remind him of Mom's orders to cheer Dad up.

"Well, one thing's sure. I've lasted longer than most because I've had two young men to help me." Dad flicked a glance to both boys and tried a smile.

Drew returned the smile. Ever since he was old enough to drive a team, Drew had grown the family's popcorn himself—first with Granddad's help, lately alone. The satisfaction he took in plowing, discing, planting, tilling, harvesting, and shucking his own crop had helped convince him that his future was on the farm.

"Yeah; well, without me—" Poke started. He broke off and rubbed vigorously at the ear of popcorn in his hand.

Mr. Ralston went on as if he hadn't heard Poke.

"And I reckon we're a mite stronger than most who've only lately come to farming. After all, we're the sons and grandsons of the pioneers who settled this country." He stroked the ear of corn.

Drew thought he saw Dad glance at Granddad's empty seat. So far, their mission had failed. He needed to change the subject.

"Uh, Dad? I'm, uh, sorry I didn't get the Man of the Year award." He looked from Dad to Poke and back to Dad. "Everybody seemed to be counting on it. . . . It was my own fault. . . ."

Outside the wind howled around the little house and poked in the gaps between the clapboards. Billy growled.

Poke said, "Well, you are the Man of the Year in my book, no matter what anybody else says."

Dad nodded. "Me, I'd say so." He looked up at Drew for a moment, and his face reddened to the same shade as his freckles. "I just don't want you to feel bad."

Drew stared at the tin pie plate balanced on his knees. With his thumbs he pushed the end kernels off his ear of corn into the plate as Granddad had taught him, then rubbed the length of the ear with a cob to loosen the rest of the kernels. "Thanks, you guys," he got out finally.

They went on working in silence. As his pie plate filled,

Drew emptied it into the graniteware kettle. For as long as he could remember, this shelling of the popcorn had been a family ritual, through good times and bad. The day Granddad died; the time Poke was injured by the falling tree while cutting firewood; the night he himself was born, Mom had said, the men in the family had passed the time by shelling popcorn.

At last Poke said, "That looks like enough for tonight, unless you want to fill the kettle like we used to."

Dad shook his head. "Better make it last. I'll hold the lantern while you winnow it."

Drew felt restless. "Think I'll check on Moxie and the others. Meet you at the house."

Billy Boy leaped to his side and hurried through the closing door after him into the hot and dusty darkness.

At the barn Moxie greeted them with a chucklelike whicker and nosed Drew's empty pockets. The mule and the dog exchanged greetings and decided to like each other.

Drew sighed and leaned his head into Moxie's neck. Tears still lurked behind his eyes, but he knew Mom had been right. Their most important work tonight was lightening Dad's mood.

By the time Drew joined his family in the kitchen, Poke nearly had the corn popped. His face shiny, he slid the cast-iron skillet vigorously to and fro on the stove top. The tiny kernels of corn exploded noisily against the heavy lid. A pan of home-churned butter melted on top of the warming oven.

Palms on the table, Dad lowered himself into his chair and winked at Mom. "Well, Mother, I'd say we raised these boys right. Drew grows it, Poke pops it, and all we do is enjoy it." His voice sounded less heavy.

From the washbasin Drew shot Mom a glance to confirm that her strategy seemed to be working.

Her laughter bubbled. "Yes, but you help shell it. For once I don't have a thing to do with it." But she bustled around the kitchen, setting out cereal bowls and glasses at each place, filling a crock with aging apples and an aluminum pitcher with cow's milk cold from the icebox.

Poke dumped the skillet of popped corn into Mom's white enamel dishpan, then scooped another slab of lard into the skillet and emptied the rest of the popcorn from the graniteware kettle. Soon the sizzle of the lard gave way to the popping of the kernels.

When all the corn had been popped and buttered, Poke, Mom, and Drew joined Dad at the table. Everyone dipped a cereal bowl into the dishpan of popcorn in the center of the table.

Drew tossed a kernel of popcorn at Poke. "Miss Jordan told us that even the ships far out at sea radio that dust is settling on their decks."

Poke flicked a piece of popcorn across the table toward Drew, but it skittered onto the floor, where Billy Boy pounced on it. "Yeah. Well, I heard the prairie dogs are digging new holes six feet in the air."

Drew grinned and chucked another kernel of corn to Billy, who caught it in the air. "Okay, wise guy. I heard the crows are flying backward to keep the dust out of their eyes."

Even Mom and Dad joined Poke's laughter.

Encouraged, Drew pressed on. "Did you hear the one

about the man that was hit on the head by a raindrop? He was so overcome that two buckets of sand had to be thrown in his face to revive him."

When their parents' knowing chuckles had subsided, Poke said, "I heard the jackrabbits have been sneezing themselves to death."

Drew grimaced. "That one ain't so funny. I seen a bunch of dead jackrabbits and birds in the fence rows coming home from Jay's. Tomorrow I'm gonna pick up some of 'em to feed the hogs."

Both he and Dad reached for the last apple in the crock at the same time.

"Go ahead," Dad said.

"That's okay. You take it."

Dad shook his head. "No, son. You can have it." He placed the apple in front of Drew. "That reminds me. Did you fellas ever turn them hogs into the alfalfa like I told you to?"

Drew and Poke exchanged glances.

"Drew said he'd do it," Poke said slowly.

Dad turned to Drew. "Well?" All merriment had left his eyes.

"Dad, that alfalfa is worth a lot more to the other stock, cut and dried, than it is to the hogs in the field—"

"I don't—" Dad's face had begun to redden.

"Please, Dad, hear me out." His arm on the table, Drew leaned toward his father. "Now, I know you can't use Rose to mow the alfalfa. But what about Moxie? He ain't in the best of condition, either, but he's young and strong and he stands the heat better than any half-starved horse."

He paused to watch the expression on Dad's face, but

could not read what he saw there. "Maybe Moxie could earn his keep by cutting the alfalfa for the stock, to tide them over a while longer."

Poke let out his breath. "You sound just like Granddad."

Dad leaned back in his chair and looked at Drew. He nodded. "Poke's right. I see your granddad in you more and more every day. And he'd be right proud." He rubbed the callus on his thumb. "Sorry as it is, the alfalfa's got to be worth far more than two dollars in feed."

Drew grinned. "I know Moxie can do it. It'll be hard on him, but we'll take it slow and easy and give him some oats."

Dad held Drew's eyes for a long moment. "Looks like I've been giving up a mite too soon."

"Then we can stay?" Drew's voice did not break. It sounded deep and manly.

Poke inspected the popcorn.

Dad sighed. "We'll see," he said. He studied Mom's hopeful face. "We'll see what the banker has to say, and then we'll see."

CHAPTER **14**

In the two weeks that school had been out, the heat and drought had not eased. Drew had struck a good deal with Clayton for the sale of his sheep; but Dad's July deadline loomed two weeks closer, still with no decision announced.

"Mrs. Davis says it's the end of the world." Mom rested in her favorite rocking chair. Her feet dangled when the chair rocked back.

Drew lounged beside Billy Boy on the concrete floor of the porch, where the heat had driven them after supper. The dust seemed no worse there than in the house.

Mom stared uneasily into the hazy distance. "She says the dust is blowing straight from hell."

Poke was sprawled on an old kitchen chair. "The dust ain't from hell. You only got to look at it and smell it to know where it's coming from." He pushed his hair off his damp forehead. "If it's brown, you can figure it's our own Kansas topsoil. If it's red, it's either from Colorado or Oklahoma. If it smells like sheep, it's Colorado. If it's yellow and tastes bitter, it's blown up from Texas or New Mexico." He brandished the flyswatter.

"My law, ain't it a sight how thick the flies and skeeters are." Mom fanned her flushed face with her apron.

Dad stirred on Granddad's daybed in the corner.

"Plague, Bea. Goes along with famine and drouth."

Mom shuddered and glanced at the chicken house. "If it don't cool off, I'm gonna have a pile of dead chickens. Oh, look—a sun dog."

Drew craned his neck. "Two of 'em, Mom. One on each side of the sun." Like pieces broken off a rainbow, each seemed to enclose its own tiny sun.

"Change in the weather," Poke predicted.

Dad yawned. "All signs fail in dry weather."

"All signs fail in Kansas." Mom sniffed. "Only fools and strangers predict weather in Kansas. My law, it's too hot even to fan. A body would think it'd cool off a little when the sun set."

She let her apron drop in her lap and shielded her eyes from the sinking sun. "I was down in the cellar today. I counted the jars. . . . I'm about out of ways to stretch them any further."

Dad shifted; the daybed springs creaked under his weight.

Drew scratched Billy Boy's ears. The dog panted hard; saliva dripped from his tongue onto the concrete floor. "Stock feed's holding out pretty good, thanks to Moxie." The spindly alfalfa hay, poor as it was, had been safely stored in the barn loft. For as long as it lasted, the stock would eat. "And Billy's earned his keep by helping with the sheep." He pushed aside the thought that after tomorrow there would be no sheep to care for.

Poke grunted. "Yeah. Well, I sure ain't earning my keep." He shoved back his chair and shambled into the house.

"Poke talks about leaving all the time," Drew pointed out.

Mom passed a hand wearily over her face. "And he coughs so much."

"My greatest fear is that he'll run off and ride the rails," Dad said.

Mom's eyes widened. "You mean become a hobo?"

"Lots of young men his age have been forced to that," Dad answered.

Drew swallowed hard. "That would take guts."

Dad's eyes met Drew's. "You may be right." His drawn face reflected the light of the dying sun. The reddish hue flamed his hair. "But it takes a hell of a lot of courage to stay."

He jerked his head at the sunset. "Look at the clouds in the west."

Drew stared. Clouds did indeed boil across the western sky. Backlit by the sun, they humped and tumbled, stampeding like a herd of ghostly buffalo across the crimson sky.

"Maybe it'll rain!" Drew glanced quickly at his father.

Dad's gaze lingered on the fence line where the dust had drifted. Nothing survived there except a few dusty sunflowers. Nothing moved but the shifting dust and the wayward tumbleweeds.

The western sky rumbled.

Mom's head snapped up. "What was that?"

"Thunder, woman," Dad said. "You forgot what thunder sounds like?"

Poke slouched in the kitchen doorway. "Was that thunder?"

Drew laughed. "Yes, thunder!" He whooped and skipped out the door.

Billy Boy crowded at his heels. The dog lifted his nose

and sniffed the wind that tugged his ears. He batted his eyes, looked at Drew, and seemed to smile.

"What is it, boy, huh? You smell the rain, huh, Bill? Whoopee!" He whirled, stumbled over a tree root in the darkness, and laughed again. "Dad, Billy thinks it's gonna rain!"

The twink of a lightning bug caught Drew's eye. He remembered how he and Granddad had caught lightning bugs in a Mason jar on hot evenings of a life that now seemed only a pleasant dream.

Dozens of lightning bugs blinked on and off, seeming to signal the real lightning that gleamed below the horizon.

Mom stood in the screen door and watched the sky. "Just heat lightning."

Dad studied the flashing signals and said, "It might be just an electrical storm."

She sighed. "An electrical storm will sour what little milk we have left."

"The cows are going dry anyway, Bea. It won't matter soon," Dad said.

Drew sobered. Their hopes for rain had been disappointed so many times.

Mom returned to her rocking chair. "We'll miss the cheese and butter money," she said to herself.

Drew peered through the screen door into the darkness of the porch. "Can we listen to the radio, Dad?"

"No, we'd best not run the batteries down. Besides, I'm going to sleep." He stretched out on the daybed with a groan.

Poke lugged his mattress across the porch and into the yard.

"Ain't you afraid you'll get wet, Poke?" Drew asked. Nightfall hid the clouds, but thunder muttered in the distance and lightning flirted above the horizon.

"Naw. Just teasing us, same as always," Poke said over his shoulder.

Drew considered. Maybe if he tempted it to rain, it would. It was too hot in the house for sleep. Defiantly he toted out his mattress. The wind felt a trifle cooler against his hot skin.

He arranged his mattress beside Poke's, then collapsed on it and studied the sky through the naked branches of Granddad's hackberry tree. They had been denied its cooling shade this nightmare spring. The few stunted leaves that ventured forth were soon sanded off by the wind-whipped dust.

He thought of the story about the tigers chasing around and around a tree until they melted into butter. He felt he must surely melt down into a pool of *something* as he chored and sweated and fought for breath in the heat.

Billy Boy flopped nearby; the dog's tongue clicked stickily as he panted. Drew reached out to him with pride and affection. Billy had taken to the sheep like a born herder.

With a pang Drew remembered again that tomorrow Uncle Clayton would truck the sheep to his place. And they would have money enough to leave the farm.

Got to talk to Dad again about using the money to stay, Drew thought. Because of the new law, the banker could only threaten and plead. But Dad still would not discuss his thinking on whether to leave anyway. Without rain, Drew admitted to himself, the land could not support them.

Thunder boomed close by, and lightning flashed a

promise. Drew crossed his fingers and stared up through the stark branches.

Intermittently he could see a line of huge thunderheads marching across the fields toward them. If only it would rain, maybe—with the sheep money—Dad would be encouraged to stay.

The smell of rain grew stronger. A sprinkle of cool raindrops on his hot face . . .

Drew snatched up his mattress and raced for the porch, shouting, "Rain! Rain!"

The wind freshened. It lifted the dust higher and wrestled with Drew for his mattress, which caught the wind like a sail and pulled him stumbling alongside.

"Hey, Poke, wake up. Better get your mattress inside."

Thunder rolled continuously now. Lightning exploded nearby. The glare stabbed Drew's dark-dulled eyes.

The sprinkle increased to a shower.

Poke sat up. The wind whipped his hair; it chased his sheet across the yard like a harried ghost.

Under the lightning flares the barren trees tossed and bent before the wind like buffalo grass. But the rain slackened.

Drew turned his face to the sky. "Rain!"

The thunder mocked him as it retreated. The precious drops ceased.

"Not enough to settle the dust," Mom whispered.

Drew dragged his mattress back to the yard. Sharp disappointment almost brought tears. He breathed the aura of heat—hot dirt, hot grass, hot wind. The parched earth had soaked up the pitiful shower without a trace.

Billy Boy licked Drew's hand and settled down again

beside him. The ground quivered to a rumble in the distance. Had the storm turned back? Drew wondered.

Presently Drew heard the panting of the steam locomotive as a long freight pulled the grade out of the creek bottom. It seemed to breathe deeply and gasp for air as it heaved the heavy cars up the hill.

Drew turned to look. The engine's headlight played on the bottoms of the clouds. He pictured the fireman desperately shoveling coal, stoking the boiler fire red hot.

A fountain of sparks spewed from the tall smokestack into the night. Gradually the train sounds faded, seeming to chase the thunder and lightning before them.

Drew dozed in the drone of thirsty insects.

Abruptly he awakened to the din of Billy's frantic barking. Puzzled, he sat up.

Lightning illuminated the night like a stroboscope. In the light of the flashes Drew saw a wisp of gray over the barn become a towering pillar of black even as he watched. Under it, flames clawed at the wind.

Lightning—or a spark from the locomotive—had ignited the tinder-dry barn roof. Billy's barking grew to a frenzy. Paralyzed, Drew stared.

"Drew, quiet that dog." Dad appeared in the screen door like a pale ghost.

Then, "My God! Bea, Poke, get up! Barn's afire!" he roared. "Bea, get the buckets and blankets. Poke, get on the pump! Danged if this ain't the last straw!"

He snatched his overalls off the daybed and hopped on one leg in his haste to struggle into them. He put both legs into one pants leg and nearly lost his balance, cursing loudly.

Lightning stabbed close by. Drew started and averted his head. He glimpsed Mom with her hand to her mouth, her eyes terrified.

A thunderclap nearly drowned Dad's shout. "Drew, help me get the stock out of the barn!" He shoved Mom out of his way and vaulted off the porch. "Move! All of you!"

As he disappeared into the darkness, Drew heard him pray, "God, don't let that well go dry!" Mom hurried after him.

Raindrops splattered in the dust momentarily, then stopped.

Billy Boy barked passionately. The barn roof blazed, rouging the black sky with an orange glow.

Dad appeared in the eerie light in the doorway, tugging desperately on Rose's halter. Panic-stricken, the mare fought his efforts to lead her away from the fire and finally broke from his grasp.

Lightning flashed again. Rose screamed, reared, and fell thrashing to the ground.

Dad barely glanced at her before dashing back inside the barn. He emerged almost instantly with another horse. Dimly visible, Mom led out a cow.

Earsplitting thunder rumbled almost continuously and overpowered the shouts of Dad and Poke. Smoke billowed across the yard. Drew wanted to hide his eyes, and his feet seemed rooted to the ground.

But he heard Moxie calling to him. And he must get his sheep out of the lean-to next to the barn.

"Drew! Bring me water! We've got to save the alfalfa!"

Moxie's brays were frantic now.

"Moxie!" He began to run for the barn. "I'm coming, boy!"

"Drew, wait!" Dad yelled. "Don't go in there—it's too far gone." He reached out and stopped Drew in his tracks.

"But, Dad! Moxie's in there!" He pulled against his father's hand.

Dad's eyes reflected the light of the flames. "I know, son, and Rose's colt . . . maybe others. But I can't risk you, too." He held Drew's shoulder with one iron hand and cupped his head with the other.

Drew looked up, felt the tears well in his eyes and spill down his cheeks before he could stop them.

Dad grimaced and the muscle worked in his jaw. "Stay here." He snatched a wet blanket from Mom and draped it over his head and shoulders, then darted through the flaming doorway into the smoke-filled barn.

Drew held his breath. When he thought his lungs must surely burst, Dad's smoking blanket reappeared in the firelit doorway.

When Dad released the mule's halter, Moxie galloped into the barnyard and sailed past Drew, his eyes wild.

Drew dashed the tears from his eyes and peered into the smoke. Dad emerged, leading Rose's colt.

Drew turned to the dog beside him. "Come on, Billy, we've got to get the sheep out!"

He shut out the smell of singed horsehair, ignored the wind-roiled dust in his eyes and the lightning all around him. He sprinted to the sheep shed and threw open the door.

Smoke billowed out. "Bo-Peep!" he called desperately. If he could get the leader moving to the door, maybe the others would follow. Judging by the heat from the barn wall at his side, he had only moments before the wall burst into flames.

"Bo-Peep!" A tongue of flame licked at the bottom of the wall, lit the shed. The flock huddled in the far corner. Billy Boy crowded beside Drew.

The fire lighted the way to Bo-Peep. Drew hauled her to her feet and wrestled her to the door and safety, but the other ewes would not follow.

Billy Boy barked a command and nipped at the nearest ewe. When she leaped to her feet, Billy hurried her to the door.

"Drew!" Mom's shout sounded close, but Drew could not see her through the smoke. "The shed's on fire! You've got to get out of here!" She threw a wet blanket across his shoulders, clutched at him, and pulled him away from the shed.

But again and again Billy Boy entered the burning shed. As soon as his encouraging nips ushered one ewe from the building, he hurried after another. His fur smoked.

Drew ran to the pump for a bucket of water and flung it over the dog the next time he emerged.

At last Billy Boy seemed satisfied all the sheep were out of the shed. He loped around the barnyard, herding the animals into a knot.

Drew hurried to open a corral gate. Unbidden, Billy worked the flock into the corral.

Heat from the burning barn joined the heat of the night. Drew's skin prickled; his mouth was parched.

The shed roof collapsed. Sparks showered into the blackness above the barn and swirled uncertainly in the shifting currents of the air.

CHAPTER **15**

Drew had not heard the car approaching, but he looked up as Uncle Clayton's Packard careered into the yard. Out of all four doors spilled cousins and hired men with pails.

Behind it bucked the neighbors' old Model T, top down. Men tumbled in the seats and clung on the running boards. They went pounding to the fire before the car stopped. The shouts and curses of the running men added to the confusion.

Clayton took Dad's arm. "I saw the glow all the way to my place," he boomed.

"Water!" pleaded Dad, his voice harsh from shouting and breathing smoke.

Clayton glanced at the burning barn and shook his head. "Well, we've got to try."

The men hastily formed a line from the pump to the barn. Filled water buckets were handed down the row to the barn in a continuous stream.

Dad and Poke and Clayton flung the water at the barn with all their might. Steam hissed and rose into the night, but the fire inched upward.

The flames illuminated the barnyard. Dad sagged against the stock tank and struggled to breathe. The whites of his eyes seemed startling in his soot-blackened face. "Let it go." His chin sank upon his chest.

Drew shouted, "No! Don't give up! The alfalfa's in there!"

But the circle of men stared helplessly at the blazing skeleton of the barn.

Drew searched the crowd for Uncle Clayton. He glimpsed his mother on the path, spotlighted in the firelight. She lifted her robe above her ankles and ran toward him. The hairpins holding the bun at her neck loosened, and her hair spilled over her shoulders and down her back. The wind caught it, and it sailed behind her. Fear and soot lined her drawn face.

Abruptly a black cat streaked across the barnyard. Not one of theirs, since Mom tolerated no black cats on their farm. He must be a stray, Drew thought, seeking shelter and dislodged by the fire.

With a shriek, Mom stopped short, as though checked by an invisible rein. But she brushed back her hair and continued her rush toward Drew.

"The lilac!" she screamed. "My lilac bush is on fire! Help me, Drew! Put it out!"

But from out of the darkness, Billy Boy threw himself at Drew's legs.

He staggered. "Hey, Bill, what's wrong with you?" He snapped his fingers and reached a hand to the barking dog. "Here, Bill, quiet now."

Billy backed away, but his barking did not cease. His eyes reflected the firelight. He darted under Drew's outstretched arm and snapped up the hem of Mom's robe, tugging so hard she nearly lost her footing.

In exasperation Drew looked to heaven for help.

Then he saw it—fire on the roof of the house. Fingers

of flame stretched over the gable and curled under the eaves. Wood shingles parched by months of heat and drought glowed red-orange almost instantly. Even as Drew watched, the flames reached out hungrily.

"The house! The roof is on fire!" He could scarcely hear his own voice over the din of the shouting, coughing bucket brigade, the barking dog, the frightened animals, the sledge-hammering thunder.

Frantically he searched for his father in the smoke and melee. He found him and tugged at his overalls. "Dad, the house! The roof is on fire!"

Dad stared at him blankly. Drew thought he would be brushed aside. "The house, Dad! A spark! The roof's on fire!"

Dad jerked around, grabbed Poke by the shoulder, and jabbed a finger. "Get the ladder from the shop," he yelled hoarsely.

Drew flew up the path to the house. He heard Dad and his helpers panting close behind. They snatched filled water buckets as they passed the pump.

Mom still stood by the charred lilac bush. She clutched a lantern and shrieked hysterically.

Dad seized her shoulders and shook her hard. "Hush, Bea! I need you if we're going to save the house! Water! Bring me water! And bring that lantern over here!"

The wildness went out of Mom's eyes. She flung her hair over her shoulder, and hastened after Poke and the ladder.

Dad had climbed halfway up the ladder when it was barely in place. Poke settled the foot firmly, and Drew struggled after Dad with a heavy bucket, water sloshing at every rung. He looked up: flames from the roof leaped high into the dark sky.

"Drew!" Dad shouted. "Hurry!"

Drew passed the bucket up to Dad, then jumped clear of the ladder. He fell to his knees and scrambled for his footing.

Behind him the bucket brigade took its place. When a full bucket was thrust in his hands, the man at the foot of the ladder mounted several rungs and passed it up to Dad. When he descended the ladder, he grabbed an empty bucket from those Dad had dropped and got in line at the pump. Two men spelled each other on the pump handle. When his bucket filled, the volunteer raced back to pass it down the line to the ladder. By then there was a man behind him with another full bucket.

Drew sagged against the broad trunk of the hackberry tree. A bucket of water made a terrible load, and he envied Poke's ability to carry two full buckets at a time.

His father balanced on the ladder, silhouetted against the flames on the roof. An angry hiss greeted each bucket of water that Dad heaved, but still the fire inched outward. Steam rose in clouds from the hot shingles, almost obscuring the top of the ladder.

Dad's mouth worked; he shouted, but the wind jerked away his words. Drew strained to hear them.

". . . attic! . . . burned through! Fire in the attic!"

Drew froze. No one else appeared to have heard. Then he spotted Poke, stumbled to him. He grasped Poke's arm and pointed at Dad, at the hole now visible in the roof, the smoke belching and mingling with the steam. "The attic," he croaked.

Understanding dawned in Poke's eyes. "The fire's in the attic!" he shouted. "Here, some of you, form a line up the steps."

He grabbed a man from the line to the ladder. "Every other man come with me." He snatched a water bucket and whirled to the porch door. "Drew, get some water up here—and some light!" The dark house swallowed him.

Mom appeared out of the blackness and plucked at Drew's shoulder. "What?" she shrieked.

Drew pointed. "The attic, Mom. The attic's burning!"

She swayed; her eyes closed.

Drew grabbed her hand. "Mom, we gotta help Poke!"

She nodded and, holding her lantern high, dashed into the house.

Drew hefted a full bucket on the run and followed her up the stairs. There was no ceiling in the attic; the burning roof had collapsed directly onto the attic floor.

Dangerously near the fire, Poke flailed at the flames with a wet gunny sack. Drew flung his bucket of water and hurried out.

On his next trip, he had only to dart to the landing for more water. The others had formed a brigade up to the top of the steps. Back and forth from the landing to the burning attic he and Mom toiled, exchanging empty buckets for full ones.

Drew's arms trembled from the effort. He thought he would surely drop, but he labored on. They had to save the house—could not be forced to leave the farm. *Must get water to Poke.*

When at last the fire yielded, steam hung in the air. In the lantern's glow, drops of water glistened on the charred boards. The stench flared Drew's nostrils. He gazed up, through the hole in the roof, into the lightning-streaked sky. All that thunder and lightning—and no rain, he thought. But the house still stood.

"I can't believe it didn't rain," Dad said when the family gathered on the screened-in porch. A single lantern had survived the wind and struggled to light the porch.

Dad ran a trembling hand through his sweat-soaked hair. "Thank God we're all okay," he said huskily. "I saw Poke headed for the stock pens."

He pulled Mom and Drew into the circle of his arms and held them for a long moment.

Drew's knees felt rubbery. He dropped into the rocking chair and grinned at his father. "Our good luck's holding."

Mom sagged to the edge of the daybed and clutched the skirt of her stained and water-soaked robe. "Are you daft, child?" Her voice shook with exhaustion and emotion. "Our barn burned to the ground, the house . . . That black cat! The lilac bush . . . On top of all our other trials . . ."

Drew shrugged. "We got the stock out. The well didn't go dry. The house has a hole in it, but it's still standing— and we're alive." He tried to cough the smoke from his lungs.

Neither the wind nor the few raindrops had eased the heat. Heavy as steam, the air was as hard to breathe. After the violence of the storm and the confusion of the fire, the silence seemed tangible.

Dad coughed and sat by Mom, swept her into his arms. "I'd feel a mite better about our luck if it had rained."

At the screen door, Billy shook the ashes from his damp fur. Dad jerked his head to the door. "Let that dog in, Drew. He's the hero of the night." He propped his elbows on his knees and rocked forward, his head in his hands. "God, I'd forgotten how much this old place means to me."

Drew fell to his knees and hugged Billy Boy. With the dog in his lap, he sat on the floor by the screen door and peered out. Black water still dripped from the eaves. He wondered if they would ever get the smell of the fire out of the house.

He staggered to his feet and crossed to the daybed. He perched on the edge beside Dad and cleared his throat. "Speaking of heroes, Dad . . . Thanks an awful lot for savin' Moxie." It seemed too little to say. "It really means a lot to me." He shrugged. "He means a lot."

Dad's arm pulled him into a rough hug. He nodded and stretched a grin. "Wish I could've saved the alfalfa, too! Losing it . . ." He broke off and dropped his head back into his hands.

Lighted lanterns appeared to float around the ruins of the barn as their rescuers gathered up buckets and belongings and began to leave. Someone he could see only in silhouette herded the rest of the stock into the pens. He did not walk like Poke.

A single rifle shot broke the muggy stillness and echoed across the plains.

Drew jumped and turned a startled face to Dad.

Mom leaped to her feet. "My law, now what's happening?"

"Clayton shot the mare—put her out of her misery." Dad's voice choked in his throat.

Drew rose and leaned his forehead against the screen.

He bit his lip to stop the tears. "Well, that's one less mouth to feed," he said.

Mom pivoted. "Where's Poke?"

The only answer was the crossing signal of an eastbound freight. Two long, one short, one long.

Despite the heat, Drew shivered. The night train to Kansas City!

The unspoken thought lingered in the air like the steam.

"Oh, my law!" Mom gasped. "He wouldn't hop that freight, would he?" She clutched Dad's overall bib. "Would he, Walt?"

Her husband got stiffly to his feet. "I couldn't say, Mother." He held the lantern aloft to light Drew's face. "Have any ideas about that, son?"

Drew forced himself to meet Dad's gaze. He squinted against the lantern light. "No, sir."

Dad grunted and went out. "I'll see if he's down at the pens." The screen door squawked, then slammed behind him.

Drew pumped a bucket of water for Billy Boy. Leaving the exhausted dog to rest on the cool concrete floor of the porch, he trailed into the blackness of the yard.

Moxie also needed water and loving pats. And since the well at the stock tank was dry, he would have to pump water for the sheep.

He wished he felt as sure of their continuing good luck as he had let on to Mom and Dad. Saving Moxie and the sheep was very good luck, but losing the alfalfa was very bad. That would scarcely help convince Dad to stay. And now even Mom doubted their future.

If only he could take back the promise to Poke not to tell

Mom and Dad of his plans to leave. There might still be time to stop him.

After hours of waiting and searching for Poke, Drew still cursed himself for making that promise.

Driven from his upstairs room by the fire damage to the attic and the heat under the eaves, he had gone to lie in Poke's bed.

"Then when he comes in, we'll know it right away," Mom had insisted.

Drew thought it unlikely that he would be able to sleep. Behind his closed eyelids the fire scene played over and over again like a serial repeated too often at the movie theater's Saturday matinee.

"Promise me!" In Drew's nightmare, Poke clutched at his throat. *"You promised me!"*

Billy Boy's whimper woke him. For a moment he lay listening to the dog's soft whining, as though he also suffered from a bad dream.

Then Drew knew that someone else was in the room. He sat bolt upright in bed. The moon peeked from behind lingering clouds and cast a shadow in the dresser's smoky mirror.

"Is that you, Poke?" Drew whispered.

"Yeah. Well, I figured you'd be in my room." He groped his way to the bed and perched on its edge.

Billy Boy went to him, and Poke fondled the dog's ears. "You didn't tell them, did you?"

Drew shook his head, then remembered Poke might not be able to see him. "Nope. But you gotta let me! We thought you were on the freight to Kansas City."

Poke shrugged. "I should be. But I lost my nerve. So then I decided to come home and clean up and get a few things. Maybe say good-bye to you." He coughed softly. "There's another train in a little bit."

"Why won't you say good-bye to Mom and Dad, Poke?"

"Can't. Mom would bawl and I couldn't stand that." He felt for Drew's arm. "And I gotta go, buddy. I gotta."

Drew took a quavering breath. "Then let—"

"No! You promised me. If you tell them, they'll come after me, or send someone else. Believe me, this is the best way. It'll hurt less in the long run."

Moonlight reflected off Poke's grin. "Make you a deal. Wait three days, time enough for me to get to K.C. and get swallowed up in the city. Then you can tell them where I am."

Drew nodded. "Okay," he agreed reluctantly. The square of moonlight on the linoleum beside the bed reminded him of the night Poke had walked home from Madsen's to keep him company with Moxie.

The far-off moan of a locomotive stiffened Poke. "I'll catch her when she slows coming up the hill from the creek." He gripped Drew's shoulder. "Take care, buddy."

Drew swallowed. "See you, Poke."

CHAPTER 16

The next morning Drew awoke with a sense of dread. He wrinkled his nose. The stench of the fire had not lessened. As usual, he could taste the dust.

Then he remembered that Clayton would take the sheep today. And that Poke had gone.

He had always thought he would be glad to see Poke go. For years he had imagined the day he would have Mom and Dad all to himself.

He fondled Billy Boy's ear, and the dog licked his hand. At first light he would need to check on Moxie and see that he had water. Mules were supposed to be able to go without water longer than anything except a camel. But Moxie drank a lot, especially when the dust blew.

The wind moaned around the side of the house, then slammed against the window.

Drew shuddered. Surely it should be light outside by now. Dawn came early to the prairie in the summertime.

He fumbled in the grit on the pine stand that Poke had made for Granddad in shop class. His fingers closed on a box of matches, and he lit the stub of candle.

Wiping the dust from the face of the clock, he tilted it to the candlelight. The clock agreed: it should be daylight.

Drew rose and peered out the window. He saw only his own reflection looking back at him.

He shook the dust out of the clean clothes Mom had found to fit him. Soot as well as dust covered his own wardrobe.

Mom's head appeared in the doorway. "Hey, slugabed, you up?" Her eyes glistened and she managed only a faint smile. "Come on in the kitchen, honey. The duster is gettin' real bad, and I 'spect it's worse in here because the wind is on this side of the house."

He shrugged. "Has Dad been out to check on the stock?"

She shook her head. Her gaze lingered longingly on Poke's room.

The wind shrieked under the eaves like a wild thing. Mom shuddered. "We're doomed. We should have left before, like your dad said."

Drew sighed. "Come on, Billy, let's go check on Moxie." He left the candle for his mother and felt his way through the unnatural darkness to the kitchen.

The smell of the fire seemed only a little less noticeable there, and the dust no better. For once the cookstove had cooled, but the room remained oven hot.

The radio played quietly on the kitchen table. Dad sat with his elbows on the table, his head in his hands. His father must be uncommonly concerned, Drew thought, or he would not run down the already-weak batteries.

". . . at your Western Auto store in Garden City." The announcer's voice sounded tired and tense.

"Near Delphos a seventy-three-year-old man named Gus Peterson went to his privy during the night, and the storm caught him there. Lost, exhausted, and bewildered, he tried in vain to crawl to his house following a fence line. The coroner reports that death was caused by suffocation. Authorities continue to recommend the use of a lifeline. . . ."

Dad straightened at the sound of Drew's step and sat stiffly erect. "You okay, son?" He peered into Drew's face.

Drew nodded. "Sure." He met Dad's red-rimmed eyes. "Are you?"

"Just trying to count my blessings."

Drew took a step toward his father, reached for him, then stopped and let his hand drop. "Dad, we can—"

Dad's gaze slid back to the radio. He held up a hand for silence.

". . . and his family were three miles in the country when overtaken by the storm. He was forced to get out of the car and feel around for fences in order to tell whether he was in the road or not, then went into the ditch three times before getting home.

"Even in town, where streetlights continue to burn at mid-morning, several motorists going home drove past their own homes in the black curtain of dust and wandered around in the yards and driveways of their neighbors trying to get into their own garages.

"Meanwhile, at local hospitals all surgery has been cancelled because the doctors' instruments cannot be sterilized. Nurses work frantically to keep patients' beds and medications free of dust, and many patients with respiratory trouble have their faces covered with dampened cloths. . . ."

"Where's your ragbag, Bea?" Dad shouted. "We've got to do something about the dust in here."

Behind Drew, Mom sniffed. "Most of it's on our backs.

I've been patching the patches for months."

She clutched a framed photograph of Poke to her breast with one hand and the quivering candle in the other.

"Then bring some sheets or something. We'll hang them over the windows and doors." When Mom had left the room, Dad fumbled in his back pocket for his handkerchief and blew his nose loudly.

". . . meetings and social functions have been cancelled, and virtually all business is suspended. Other than drugstores, most business houses are closed." The announcer's voice threatened to trail off.

Drew pictured the man sitting in his dusty studio, reading the news like the voice of doom. He leaned against the edge of the table and stared at the radio.

"And now the weather. Although the bad storm of last Friday night had abated somewhat, the atmosphere has been filled with dust for days. A new storm swept in from the southwest before two o'clock this morning and has been growing steadily worse.

"But while we are taking our weather straight, the dust is adulterated in other sections of the state with drops of rain to break the monotony. Rain started falling through an intense dust cloud at Hutchinson at six o'clock this morning, forming mud balls, according to a report we received over the private wire of the grain dealers here.

"At Goodland, according to the Associated Press, rain mixed with dust is driving in on a high north wind. Old-timers say this is the worst storm ever recalled here. . . ."

"Rain!" Drew burst out.

Dad waved him to silence.

". . . virtually all traffic has been halted," the radio announcer went on. "The Kansas Highway Patrol has closed most highways to await a lull in the storm, when bulldozers will attempt to clear them of dust. Bus passengers and tourists are being held here since shortly after midnight, and trains are proceeding with difficulty. . . ." A burst of static interrupted.

Trains! Drew dropped into a chair and leaned closer to the radio, his heart pounding. Poke had clearly headed right into trouble. He was glad Mom had not heard.

Static popped and crackled. The voice grew fainter. Frantically Dad twisted the dials.

" . . . dismal news this morning, folks. Stay tuned; we will bring you up-to-date reports as they become available. We return you now to our regular programming."

Dad sighed. "Sounds like we're in for it. Better get battened down. I knew I should've nailed some tin over that hole in the roof last night."

Drew hurried to the window, but still could not penetrate the envelope of dust that hissed against the glass. He tossed Billy Boy a dingy biscuit from the pie safe and pocketed one for himself. They both needed a drink of water to wash down the dust.

"Have you been out to the stock, Dad?" he asked.

Dad ran a hand over the stubble on his chin and shook his head. "But we do need to go before the dust gets any deeper against the door and we can't get out. Grab that shovel on the porch and we'll clear it away as we go."

He lifted down the coil of rope hanging on the hooks behind the door. "And we'll have to make us a lifeline or we might not find our way back to the house." He tied one end of the rope to the pitcher pump at the sink.

"Here, you two." Mom hustled back into the kitchen. "I want you to wear masks over your faces out there—and don't stay out long." She dipped muslin rags into the water bucket and tied them around their faces. "These might help a little."

Perspiration shone on Dad's forehead. "Don't worry, Bea. We're only going to fill the stock tank and clear the dust from the door. We won't be gone any longer than we have to." Dad's mask muffled his voice. "I've already lost one son. I sure won't risk this one." His eyes met Drew's over their masks. "Mother, why don't you wet down some sheets to hang over the windows. We'll grab another bucket of water on the way back."

Mom crumpled in tears. "I knew it would come to this. All those bad omens, all those bad luck spells . . ."

"Hush, Bea. There aren't that many black cats, broken mirrors, or ladders in Kansas." His hand fell on Drew's shoulder. "Come on, son. Let's get it over with."

"Sure." Drew's voice cracked; the word came out like a croak. That had not happened in a while, but nobody laughed.

"Cheer up, Mom," he said with more spirit than he felt. "The radio said it's raining someplace. Maybe that's a good omen."

"When I woke up this morning I hoped the fire was a nightmare. And Poke bein' gone . . . He's so young, just a boy really, and so weak. . . ." She rocked to and fro on the edge of her chair.

Dad pulled down his mask and squatted by her chair. "Please, Mother, you got to get ahold of yourself. I need you to be strong. Drew needs you." He gripped her hand and slid an arm around her.

Mom nodded and fumbled in her apron pocket for a handkerchief.

The soft babble from the radio changed pitch. A telegraph key chattered urgently.

Mom hunched over the instrument and fine-tuned the dials. The announcer's voice became clearer.

". . . Pacific Railroad reports the derailment early this morning of an eastbound freight train. Dust piled high between the rails derailed the front truck of the engine as the train rolled east on the trip from Salina to Kansas City.

"A wrecker was dispatched from Salina, but the severe dust this morning has halted . . ." The voice sounded as though it came through a tin can.

A kerosene lamp burned on the table, but Drew could scarcely see Mom's stark face through the dust in the room. He crossed to the table and put down a hand to steady himself, straining to understand the muffled words.

". . . delays on other lines while crew members wearing goggles and respirators walk the rails ahead to determine whether drifted dust is piled high enough to cause another derailment . . ."

A piercing whistle filled the room, and Billy Boy howled in pain. Drew quieted the dog while Dad leaped to the table and worked the radio dials with both hands. Words came in snatches.

". . . spokesman for . . . road tells us . . . wrecking crane is being readied at . . . and that extra engines with snow plows are being prepared to clear the dust drifts from the tracks." The voice faded. Only a static hiss remained.

Dad dropped into a chair and desperately screwed the dials. His fist banged the rounded top of the cabinet.

Mom sobbed.

Very faintly Drew heard, ". . . planes still grounded, of course. The weather bureau reports the wind is dropping, and judging by reports from other stations, we can expect some letup in the near future. However, reports from . . ."

Silence. Not even the crackle of static. The batteries had gone dead.

"Dad, what if Poke's on that train?" Drew asked.

Mom moaned and swayed on the edge of her chair. "He is. I know he is. And him with that awful cough. He's still so weak from the flu. He can't stand . . ." Her words became soft babbling as she cried.

"We can't know that," Mr. Ralston said.

Drew hesitated. He had *promised.* "I . . . Poke is on that train, Dad. I dreamed it."

"That's nonsense."

"No, Dad, listen." He licked his parched lips. "Last night I dreamed about Poke, and I dreamed . . ."

Mom gasped. "Hush, Drew. You mustn't tell a dream before breakfast or it will come true."

Drew forced a grin. "That's okay, Mom. I dreamed Poke hopped a train—that train—and that it derailed, and me and Dad went and found it and got Poke and brought him home." He rushed it out before he lost his nerve. Poke's leaving did seem like a dream—a nightmare.

Dad ran a freckled hand through sandy hair streaked with gray. His wife turned to him. "Walt, maybe . . ."

Dad's eyes stopped her. "I'm not going to traipse around

the countryside in a duster on some wild-goose chase."

"But, Dad! The radio said the dust is letting up, and the derailment isn't that far from here. We could take the car and be there . . ."

Dad placed his callused palms on the tabletop and heaved to his feet. "I don't want to hear any more. Poke thinks he's old enough to make his own decisions. Whether we like it or not, he decided to leave." He jerked his head toward the glimmer of delayed dawn at the window. "We'd best see to the stock."

As he chored, Drew avoided looking at the pile of smoking rubble that had been the barn. He told himself he should be glad to be free of Poke. Maybe Dad would even like him better with Poke out of the way.

When the dust finally eased, he sat on the corral fence, Billy Boy at his feet, and watched Moxie stretch his legs by galloping freely in circles.

But now Poke might be hurt in the train derailment. At best he had been caught unprepared for the monster duster. Drew felt himself to blame; he should have told Dad right away. He should tell him now.

But he had promised not to.

Poor Poke. A derailed boxcar was no place to sit out a dust storm—especially if he was hurt. Mom might believe in omens and dreams, but Dad would not be budged.

Maybe he should tell his father the truth and get help to Poke and then worry about breaking his promise. Maybe Poke's safety was more important than keeping the promise.

But Uncle Clayton said a man's word was his bond.

And Poke had left because he fancied himself a burden.

He would not appreciate Drew calling out the rescue troops at the first sign of trouble.

If they left the farm now, Poke might never find them again, Drew thought. Then he realized that Uncle Clayton would still be here. Poke could always find them through Uncle Clayton.

At the thought of Clayton, Drew struck his fist on his knee. There had been no mention of Uncle Clayton in his promise to Poke.

He would not wait for Uncle Clayton to come for the sheep. Nothing was as important as saving Poke.

Drew slipped off the gate and whistled a signal to Moxie. "Hey, you old scalawag, come here! Playtime is over."

Billy Boy stood at his heels, his tail waving in the wind.

But Moxie eluded Drew's grasp. He rolled in the drift of dust near the center of the corral. Finally he heaved to his feet, shook the dust from his mane, and frisked around the fence to Drew's side. He nuzzled Drew's pocket.

"Not this time, boy. Come on. We got to get to Clayton's before the dust hits again." He grasped the mule's halter and tugged gently.

Moxie planted his feet and refused to follow.

"Come on, jughead, this ain't no time to get stubborn." Drew tugged more insistently.

The mule tried to toss his head, but Drew held tightly to the halter. Moxie eyed him a moment longer, then followed him docilely out of the corral.

Drew glanced at the house and studied the plan forming in his mind. Since they had been up so late mopping up after the fire and fighting the dust, Mom and Dad were probably napping now, taking advantage of the lull to get some rest.

But even they admitted he was growing up. It was high time that he, too, started making some of his own decisions.

He would ride Moxie to Uncle Clayton's, tell him that Poke had hopped the night freight to Kansas City after the fire—and that the train now lay somewhere between Salina and K.C. in a dust dune. Clayton would know what to do, and Drew's promise to Poke would be unbroken.

As he had expected, Drew found a newly repaired and oiled bridle in the shop, but his saddle had burned with the barn. Grabbing a handful of Moxie's mane, he swung up on the broad bare back. Moxie snorted his complaint but took off at a stiff-legged trot, Billy Boy at his heels.

But even as he rode up the lane at Clayton's place, Drew knew his plan had failed. Not even Clayton's dog appeared at the shuttered house. The dirty Packard was gone.

The family had probably taken refuge from the duster with Aunt Martha's town relatives, who at least had running water and an indoor bathroom.

Drew threw a leg over Moxie's back and slid to the ground. Billy Boy crowded against him. The dog did not like to be separated from him even for a few minutes.

The wind pushed against Drew's cap and whipped dirt into his eyes. He tasted the grit between his teeth. He did not need the radio to tell him that the dust was not yet through with them.

He squatted and drew lines in the dust on the ground, railroad tracks cutting through the hills of dust, shortcuts from here to Poke. Could he make it alone? Could he get back before the duster struck again?

"Can't, can't, can't," echoed in his brain.

He pictured his mother, hands on her hips, her black

eyes snapping. "Can't never did anything," she lectured.

He was not sure of the distance to the derailed train, but he had recognized the name of the town nearest the accident and remembered going there with Dad. It had not seemed a long way.

The derailment would not be hard to find. All he had to do was follow the railroad tracks. Even if the duster hit again, he could stay between the steel rails all the way to the train. With Moxie's keen hearing and strong back and Billy's nose and sense of direction, nothing could go wrong.

Billy Boy pressed close and licked Drew's face. He hugged the dog to him. "The three of us ought to make a pretty good team."

Already it was past noon. If he had any hope of getting back before dark, he must leave now. He should not be gone long enough to need provisions.

"Now's when I could use some good luck," he told Billy Boy.

A gust of wind caught him and turned his head from the stinging grit. Billy's ears blew back against his head. The wind had picked up.

Dust filled the air as Drew gathered up Moxie's reins. The mule fought the lead and wanted to turn tail to the stinging wind. He twisted his neck around and bit the air beside Drew.

"You better not, jughead." Drew grinned, swung onto the mule's broad back, and swatted his rump. He whistled for Billy to follow and urged Moxie into a trot down the lane.

At the road he turned on Moxie's back and looked over his shoulder. He could not see the house through the dust.

CHAPTER **17**

Head down, Moxie plodded, his hooves plopping softly in the dust between the rails. He lifted his feet over the crossties in a broken rhythm that jarred Drew's teeth and his back. But he dared not risk leaving the tracks.

It seemed they had been under way for hours, but he had lost track of time and had no idea how far they had come. He could see only a few feet ahead, but the tracks led on.

The light seemed to be failing, and he hoped it was only a dusty twilight, not the approach of real darkness.

While the lack of a saddle had not seemed important for the short ride to Uncle Clayton's, now it loomed as a major mistake. Moxie's sweat mingled with Drew's own, and the mule's motion under the dampened seat of his overalls chafed the skin on his buttocks and thighs.

Moxie stumbled, caught himself. Billy Boy could probably use some rest, too.

"Whoa, Moxie." Drew pulled him up and dismounted.

The mule turned slightly so that the wind was at his back, lowered his head nearly to the ties, and closed his eyes. Drew flexed his legs to unkink his knees and squatted on a steel rail in its icing of dust.

Billy dropped down under Moxie's belly and rested his head on his front paws. His eyes never left Drew.

"Pretty smart, Bill. Old Moxie does make a good roof,

doesn't he?" Drew grinned at the dog and was rewarded with a flick of Billy's tail.

Drew untied and shook out his handkerchief mask. He cursed himself for not bringing water for Moxie and Billy—a more important error than riding with no saddle.

Dad would say he had gone off half-cocked. Perhaps he should simply admit that he was unprepared for the job at hand, that he was not man enough. . . .

He dropped his head in his hands and closed his eyes. They felt as if sandpapered. For the past several miles nagging thoughts had been worrying his mind like a dog does a bone. What if Poke wasn't on this train after all? What if Dad was right about this being a wild-goose chase? What if he was risking his life, probably—and Billy's and Moxie's—for nothing?

And what if he ran into another mean hobo, or a whole camp of them? What if he froze in fear as he had when the barn caught fire?

The dust eddied around them; the wind had shifted again. The silence was eerie.

He wiped his sweaty brow with the handkerchief and resettled his cap. If you bite it off, chew it, Granddad had often reminded him.

"Well, team, reckon we better keep moving. Sit in one place too long, we're apt to get buried." He replaced his mask and rose woodenly.

In a flash Billy Boy stood at Drew's side. But the dog lifted his nose, batted his eyes at the dust, and sniffed the wind. A low growl vibrated in his throat.

"Hey, Bill, what's wrong? What gives, fella?" Drew's heart pounded in his throat. He might not be as lucky with another tramp, out here in the open with no weapon.

Moxie's head jerked up; he tossed the reins. His big ears flicked like a jackrabbit's. He curled his lip and brayed. The raucous sound echoed weirdly in the otherworldly atmosphere.

Drew glanced quickly around, but a curtain of dust blocked his view. Hurriedly he gathered up the reins and vaulted astride the mule. Billy and Moxie said it was down the track, whatever it was.

"Get up! Come on, Billy!"

Moxie swung into a trot and Billy Boy moved out ahead of them.

It was the train. They had been very near the wreckage without seeing it. Like a child's toy, the railroad cars sprawled across the ghostly landscape for as far as Drew could see.

No wonder the engine had derailed. Dust had drifted into the narrow cut of a low hill and filled the tracks like snow. The rails were no longer visible, and in some places the dust had deepened enough to bury the roadbed.

Drew slowed the mule to a walk and squinted into the dust. Cars scattered along the drifted-in tracks like tumbled blocks. Thirsty cattle bawled from a still-upright stock car, but he saw no other sign of life.

He reined up beside a tilted boxcar and slid off the mule. "Wait here, Billy," he ordered. "Stay."

Drew pulled down his handkerchief mask and swiped at the dust and sweat on his face with his sleeve. He took a deep breath and hoisted himself gingerly through the narrowly opened door onto the rough floor of the boxcar.

He paused to let his eyes adjust to the gloom inside the

car. The lingering aroma of wheat reminded him that it had been a long time since his breakfast biscuit. But there was also the odor of unwashed men and sweat.

"Poke!" Drew's voice echoed in the empty boxcar. When there was no answer, Drew dropped to the ground. Hands on hips, he stared at the chaos around him.

"How in the world am I ever going to find Poke?" he said aloud.

Billy's ears perked.

Drew's heart leaped. "Hey, Bill, can you find Poke?" At the sound of Poke's name, Billy's ears lifted again.

"Sure you can! Find Poke, Billy." He flung out his arm in the same signal as when herding the sheep. "Go find Poke!"

Billy Boy cocked his head and searched Drew's face.

"Go on, Billy," Drew urged, "Moxie and me will be right behind you. Go find *Poke.*" He mounted the mule and waited.

Billy moved hesitantly toward the derailed cars. He glanced back over his shoulder.

Drew swung his arm. "That's right, Bill. Find Poke. Go get Poke."

Billy took off at a run for the sprawling cars. He began to systematically search each one with his nose.

"Atta boy, Billy!" Drew encouraged him. "That's the ticket. Good dog!" He urged Moxie after the dog, who worked quickly now, sure of his mission.

An oil car had upset but did not seem to be leaking. Hundreds of bales of hay remained intact in an overturned boxcar, but a top-heavy load of canned peas and peaches had not been so lucky. Their cardboard cases had broken and spewed cans along the tracks. A load of scrap iron homesteaded a new junkyard, and some coal cars had joined it.

When Billy Boy nudged a splintered board on the side of a boxcar, a fountain of seed corn spouted into the dust. The dog leaped back in alarm and looked to Drew for reassurance.

"Careful there, Bill. Take it easy, now. You know you won't find Poke in a full car. Look for the empties, Billy. Go on, go find Poke!"

The dust sighed and began to move again. Drew wondered about the engineer and the fireman and brakeman. They had no doubt hiked out when the duster let up. He thought of the engineers who waved to him as their trains passed through the farm.

As Drew moved slowly alongside the wreckage of the freight, he strained to see through the dust. A flatcar loaded with telephone poles tilted precariously. Its load had shifted, loosening the heavy rope restraining it and allowing most of the poles to scatter like so many toothpicks.

He threaded the mule among pieces of farm machinery thrown from their platform by the force of the impact with the car ahead. Already the blowing dust seemed determined to bury the evidence. Hundreds of milk and cream cans tumbled along the track bed.

Through the open door of another boxcar he glimpsed four brand-new automobiles chained upright, noses down. The cars appeared undamaged, and he thought guiltily of the banker's new Hudson.

The sound of Billy's frantic barking brought Drew to

attention. Keeping his head toward the car and his eye on the door, the dog circled the caboose—one of the few cars still on the tracks.

As Drew moved alongside the caboose, an embankment protected him from the wind and visibility improved. A dust dune against the side of the car hid its wheels. The fickle wind teased the drift and began to change its shape. Miniature cyclones of dust whirled into the air and swept away from the caboose.

Drew turned on Moxie's back to look. The surface of the dune rippled and eddied and reminded him of a picture he had seen of a sandy beach. The wind shaped the dust the same way it did that white sand.

Billy Boy's barking had not ceased, and his voice sounded hoarse.

"Hey, Bill, its okay now. Quiet." Drew whistled his come-to-me command and urged Moxie forward.

He swallowed to dampen his parched throat. "Poke!" he shouted. "Poke, are you in there?" His voice echoed along the cut, but he heard no other answer.

He dismounted and tied the mule's reins to the ladder on the end of the car. Billy touched his nose to Drew's leg and looked up into his face. He panted hard.

"Good dog, Billy!" He leaned and patted the dog's shoulder.

He moved around the end of the caboose and began to wade through the dust along its side. The skin prickled on his neck.

Billy Boy crowded his legs and growled a warning. The dog's teeth bared in a snarl, and the fur on his back stood erect.

Drew smelled the same peculiar odor of the tramp in the kitchen and the same fear washed over him. He heard a sound behind him.

"Youngster, be you alone?" a strange voice rasped.

Drew's heart pounded. He whirled and looked into a toothless face that loomed in the strange twilight.

"Well, did you bring help or not?" the hobo demanded. His ragged beard was grizzled with gray. He advanced to within a few feet of Drew and stopped, his watery gaze on the snarling dog.

"I'm looking for my brother," Drew stammered. "His name is Poke—or Arval. He has red hair and freckles. Have you seen him?" Nightmarish memories of the struggle in the kitchen crowded in. He fought the urge to run. Billy Boy rumbled at his knee.

The old man's hazy eyes narrowed. "You ain't no roadie. What are you doing here?" It seemed an effort to speak.

"I think my brother might be on this train." He steeled his voice. He had not come all this way to be scared off by a hobo. "My dog . . . Is Poke in this car?"

The tramp snorted. "He *might* be in Nebraska, sonny."

Drew half turned to the caboose, anxious to search for Poke, but afraid to turn his back on the tramp.

"Say, sonny, can't you hush that dog? Did you bring any food and water?" The hobo took a step toward him.

Billy Boy's growl pitched higher and louder.

A voice from the shadows within the car said, "Shut that dog up, kid, so I can think."

Drew peered into the gloom inside the car. He was separated from the half-open door by a small platform just outside it and caught only a glimpse of the man inside.

A figure reclined against the wall just inside the door, lanky legs stretched out in front of him.

"Here, Billy, quiet now," Drew commanded. "It's all right. *Quiet.*" The dog fell silent, but he did not take his eyes from the old hobo.

Drew stared at the tramp in the caboose. He seemed not much older than Poke, and a blond beard fuzzed his chin. One eye was as red as beefsteak.

"Ain't polite to stare, kid," the young bum drawled.

Drew swallowed. "Have you seen my brother?" He shot a glance back to the old man.

"Young Tennessee took a hot cinder in the eye yesterday coming out of Salina." The grizzled hobo licked his parched lips. "You got any grub, boy?"

Drew shook his head. Darkness might be near, and he still had not found Poke.

The wind moaned through the gap in the hill. The dust threatened to blow again.

Tennessee studied him out of his good eye. "What's your moniker, kid?"

Drew blinked. "Sir?" The youth's burned eye sickened him, but he held its gaze.

"Your name, idjit! What do we call you?" the grizzled one snapped.

Drew shrugged. "Ralston. Please, have you seen my brother. He's about your age, Mr. Tennessee, and—"

Tennessee cut him off. "It's him all right, Grizzly."

The two tramps exchanged looks. The older man nodded.

Tennessee coiled his long legs and stood up. Sweat glistened on his face. "Well, Ralston, your brother's in here, all right. But he's sleeping. He's been sleeping most of the time since the wreck. He don't feel so good."

Drew clanged up the iron steps to stand on the little porch outside the door.

But still Tennessee blocked the way. "You brought no water, no food. . . . What'd you think you'd do if you found Poke, tell him a bedtime story?" he asked, his voice thick with contempt.

"I didn't think."

"You sure as hell didn't," Grizzly agreed. He started up the steps behind Drew, muttering to himself.

Billy Boy advanced stiff legged toward the caboose. A warning rattled in his throat. His teeth gleamed in the unnatural light.

"You're real brave, ain't you, Ralston, with that dog backing you up," Grizzly muttered.

Drew glanced at Billy. "Sure. And you better remember one thing—his bite's a whole lot worse than his bark."

From inside the caboose Drew heard Poke's coughing. "Drew? Is that really you?"

Drew pushed past Tennessee into the darkened interior of the car. He found Poke by moving toward the sound of his coughing and knelt beside him. Billy Boy clicked across the wooden floor and pressed against Drew's back.

Poke lay stretched out on a bunk in the corner. As Drew grew accustomed to the gloom in the caboose, he searched his brother's face. With a shock he saw where Poke's eyebrows had been singed by the fire. It seemed impossible that it was only last night.

"What the heck are you doing here?" Poke whispered with effort.

Drew stared at the planked floor. "I want you to come home, Poke. Mom and Dad are real worried. . . ."

"Water," Poke whispered, his voice raspy. "Did you bring water?"

Drew shook his head sadly. "I didn't think to bring water." He could use a long, cool drink himself. "I just had to know if you were okay."

Billy barked once, a short, sharp warning.

Drew looked up to find Grizzly leaning over them. "Feelin' any better, Poke?"

Drew's head jerked up. "Trains carry water," he shouted on his way to the door.

"Whoa, youngster," Grizzly called. "If you're headed for the tender, we already thought of that. But that car dumped, and most of the water leaked out. We've already finished off what little was left." He pointed to the tin can on the floor beside Poke.

Drew bit his lip. Poke needed a drink. What else would be on the train?

"Peaches!" he cried.

CHAPTER **18**

"You about ready, Poke? We better get started before it gets dark and the wind gets worse." Drew worried that Poke had not yet agreed to the return trip.

Using the potbellied stove for support, Grizzly hauled himself off the gritty floor. "I'm getting too old to bunk on my ear."

He grimaced, exposing his toothless gums. "Me and Tennessee will stay with the train." He scratched his beard. "And you better figure on waitin' it out here with us. That snowplow will make it in tomorrow for sure, and the crane won't be far behind him."

Tennessee nodded. "Besides, Poke isn't strong enough to walk out of here in this heat." He drained the last of the juice from a can of peaches and reached for another.

Drew sighed. An hour ago they had seemed delightfully tasty, but now he thought he would never want to see another can of peaches. "He doesn't have to walk. He can ride Moxie."

Grizzly snorted. "That's even worse."

Drew opened another can of peaches with his pocket-knife and set it on the floor in front of Billy Boy. The dog needed liquid, but he had no water to offer.

Billy sniffed the peaches. He began to lap the juice without taking his gaze from Tennessee.

Tennessee laughed hoarsely. "Dogs sure don't like us 'boes. But the little ones, the terriers, are the worst. And bulldogs."

Drew shrugged. The young hobo seemed cleaner than Grizzly, but no less ragged. The tattered overalls stretched over his lanky frame seemed a few sizes too small.

Tennessee dabbed at his burned eye with a filthy handkerchief. "Well, don't know where we're going, but anywhere has got to be better than where we've been," he said.

Another of Moxie's earsplitting brays broke the eerie silence on the dust-drowned prairie. He still resented being left outside, tied to the grab bar on the porch of the caboose.

Drew laughed and rose stiffly from the bench. "Moxie wants some peaches, too." He dreaded the trip home, but every moment he lingered multiplied the risk to getting back safely. He rummaged in the broken carton for another can of peaches. "He might eat some of these things, or at least drink the juice." His sore backside made every step tortuous. The caboose swayed on its wheels as he made for the door.

"You really should stay with the train until help gets here," Grizzly said when Drew returned. "From the looks of the sky, another duster's gonna blow in here any minute."

Drew clambered up the ladder to the crow's nest and peered through the dirt-opaqued glass at the desertlike landscape. Heat waves shimmered over the steel tracks and dust devils danced among the cinders.

A coppery glow overhead could mean only one thing. The trip home would be a race with the duster. He backed down the ladder on shaky knees and worked to keep his voice light. "Better get started, Poke," he repeated.

Poke cleared his throat. "No, you better stay here until after the dust clears." He glanced at Drew and then away. "I'm staying with the train."

"No, Poke! You've got to come home with me." His voice threatened to break.

Poke shook his head. "Nothing has changed, little brother. There's nothing for me back there." He avoided Drew's eyes.

"But you're too weak to go on, too sick." Drew squatted beside Poke's bunk. He picked at the rough, dust-filled blanket and tried to swallow the lump in his throat.

Poke looked at Drew at last. "I'll be okay once I get all the smoke coughed out of my lungs. You better stay here, too. You're five miles from home with no water. When help comes we'll go to the nearest town and call Dad to come after you."

Drew sagged against the bunk. He searched Poke's face and sensed that his brother would not be moved. Time now to face the grown-up facts.

Neither Moxie, to whom a gallon was but a swig, nor Billy Boy could last long in this heat on peach juice. Another duster appeared to be bearing down on them, and the rescue crew might not make it tomorrow, either, and maybe not the next day. He had dragged Billy and Moxie into this. Now it was up to him to get them out of it.

"Granddad always said a man has to do what he thinks is right, Poke. If you have to go on, I guess you have to. But I've got to take Billy and Moxie home, same as I got here."

He held Poke's gaze. "And Poke, I want you to let me

out of my promise not to tell Dad," he said, surprised to hear his voice fill the caboose like a man's.

Poke nodded. "Yeah. Well . . ." He ruffled Drew's curls and lifted himself on one elbow. "Listen, buddy. Dad's gonna stick it out on the farm as long as he can."

Drew shook his head and started to speak.

Poke lifted a hand and hurried on. "Yeah, he is. He told me so last night, right after the fire was out. While he was still up there on the roof, he said he realized how much he cared about the place. And that he wouldn't leave until they threw him off." The last words were racked with coughing.

Drew's heart leaped in joy, then subsided. "And that's why you lit out? Because Dad said he wasn't leaving?"

Poke sank back to the cot. "You got it."

Drew sought Poke's eyes. "The radio said it rained at Hutchinson today, and some other place. That's a good sign, isn't it? Don't you think that's a good sign, Poke?"

"Sure, buddy." Poke grinned. "Your luck must be about to change." He gripped Drew's wrist. "Stay with the tracks and take care, little brother. And don't worry—you're growing up, all right. Next time I see you, you'll be a man for sure." He tried a grin, but his Adam's apple bobbed.

Drew nodded but did not move.

"Go on, now," Poke said gently, and jabbed Drew's shoulder. "Maybe you can still beat the duster."

Grizzly cleared his throat. "Personally, son, I think you've got less chance than a man with two wooden legs in a forest fire."

Drew got slowly to his feet and looked down at Poke. He shrugged. "I'm not the only one."

Poke took Drew's hand in a firm handshake. "I'll be

home someday. Remember the drugstore still owes me a mug of root beer."

Drew replayed the conversation over and over in his mind as he rode. He could think of nothing else he might have said to convince Poke to come home.

Moxie had galloped until he tired. Now he alternately walked and trotted. Billy Boy lagged behind, but was never out of Drew's sight.

Drew tried to pierce the veil ahead. A dark cloud hung there, though he could not guess how far away it was. Perhaps it stood between them and home and perhaps not. No need to get between the steel rails yet; it was easier for the mule to stay off the roadbed as long as possible.

The air seemed tinged with a sickly yellow-green. Without shadows Drew found it impossible to gauge the time, but instinct suggested that nightfall was not far off.

Except for the unbearable heat, he would doubt the sun still hung in the heavens. Nothing looked familiar, but the dust storms had so changed the countryside he wondered if he would know his own farm when he came to it.

How he wished he had not neglected to bring water! And if he ever got off this stiff-legged mule's back, he would think twice about ever riding him again. Even if they got home safely, he probably would not be able to sit down for a week. His stomach rumbled.

He began to worry about what to say to Dad. At first it had seemed simple enough, but it had never occurred to him that Poke would refuse to come home. He had thought Dad would be so glad to have Poke back that he would forget to be angry.

In the silent, eerie twilight it felt as if they were the only ones left alive. Even Moxie's hoofbeats were dust muffled. The choked plains around them seemed haunted by the ghosts of starved and suffocated cattle and birds and coyotes and by the dried-up rivers and wells and wheat.

But the worst specter was of leaving the farm: the Oakland, piled high with what little they had left, rolling slowly down the lane into the unknown. He shivered despite the heat. Even if Poke was right about Dad staying, he knew there were no guarantees. But if the rains came . . .

A sudden gust of wind whipped dust into his eyes. A dust devil sprang up ahead of the mule. Moxie snorted and broke his stride.

Drew gripped hard with his knees to keep his seat. "Easy, fella," he murmured. "You oughta be used to a little dust by now."

Moxie tossed his head, rolled the bit in his mouth, and came to a halt.

Drew sighed. "Okay, I guess we do need to rest awhile." He slid from the mule's bare back, dropped the reins, and turned to speak to Billy Boy.

The dog panted heavily. For some reason the image came to Drew's mind of Jay and his rifle that day in the Justices' barn. He sat cross-legged on the ground and hugged Billy to his side. "Wish I had a drink for you, fella."

He shook his head. All his decisions had been bad ones.

Sticking so close to the railroad tracks was costing them valuable time. Every minute in the dust posed danger to all of them. Maybe they could not last all the way home.

But if they left the tracks and struck out across country directly for home—a much shorter distance—they might end up walking in circles or missing the farm altogether.

Common sense argued that Moxie and Billy Boy could find their way home even in the dust. But he had seen them both show a tendency to turn tail and drift with the wind because that was easier.

Time to make another decision.

His weariness weighed on him. Maybe he could think more clearly if he rested. He let his gritty eyelids close at last.

No. He had made that mistake before. And if he went to sleep now, they might all die on the spot. He forced his eyes open.

The wind picked up, and the dust began to move and dirty the air.

Drew pulled up his dirt-stiffened handkerchief mask, but not soon enough to prevent a mouthful of grit from grinding between his teeth. He tugged his hat as low as it would go, narrowed his eyes to peepholes. Already they teared and burned.

His heart lurched. No matter how far they were from home, it might as well be a thousand miles. They must stay with the tracks.

He led Moxie between the steel rails of their lifeline. If he had been more than a few steps from it, it would have been hard to find.

Billy Boy crowded his legs closely. His sides still heaved and his eyes mirrored his exhaustion. Lack of water and food and breathing dust were taking their toll.

Drew knew that, just as he would never have found Poke without Moxie and Billy, he would never get home without them.

Moxie plodded blindly. Drew depended on the steel rails

to keep him on the track. He wondered if, since in some places the rails were overflowing with dust, Moxie might simply walk across one without being aware of it.

He tried to get his bearings, but the dust forced his head down. He turned up his collar to ease the stinging on his neck.

He had no way of knowing how much time had passed or how far they had walked. The world had shrunk to a few inches of visibility and his awareness of Moxie under him and Billy Boy behind him.

He felt a world away from the farm in this alien land of blowing dust. Granddad would never have believed it. Or had he foreseen it?

Granddad had preached against plowing the prairie. Nature had intended the prairies for pastureland, he insisted, and until his death had allowed only the cutting of prairie hay on what was left of his virgin land.

But Dad had broken the sod, plowed it for wheat when the market begged for more and the price of the precious grain stayed high and held out bright promises. And year after year he and the other wheat farmers, needing more and more wheat to pay the bills and buy the newfangled tractors and trucks, had plowed farther and farther into the prairie, laying it open to the mercy of the wind.

Then had come the terrible, years-long drought. The plowed ground had blown away.

Drew licked his parched lips. He knew one thing for sure. Granddad would do whatever it took to stay on the Ralston land. He would not only sell the sheep; he would sell his gold watch, his silver pocketknife, or his prize stallion.

"Pay attention now," Drew told himself aloud. Everything depended on keeping his wits. His eyes were not much help. They must be protected from the sandblasting dust. And his ears felt full of dirt.

With an occasional glance over his shoulder, Billy Boy moved out ahead and picked up the pace. Drew tried to blot out everything except the need to stay on Moxie's back and to keep the steel tracks in sight.

A clap of thunder exploded overhead.

Drew jumped as if he had been shot, causing Moxie to shy. Billy Boy barked and lifted his head, scenting the air.

Drew's heart leaped. But he had known it to thunder in a duster.

He peered from under his cap. Towering monstrously over the wide expanse of prairie, the dark cloud ahead appeared to reach out to engulf them, its top flattening like an anvil.

A flash of lightning jagged to the ground beneath the anvil, and thunder rolled toward them.

Drew gasped. Even though the freshening wind stirred the dust around Moxie's legs and stung his face, the breeze felt cooler. And moist.

Billy Boy's bark turned joyous. Moxie lifted his nose and brayed triumphantly, his big ears flicking in rhythm as he broke into a trot.

After a moment Drew whooped. Even he could smell the rain ahead. Rather than a duster, they were heading straight toward a thunderstorm.

Then Moxie whickered and voluntarily quickened his pace to a gallop. Billy raced back to Drew's side, barking and jumping like a puppy.

Drew understood. Home. They were coming home. Through the wind-whipped dust he could just make out the grove of cedars where Granddad rested, then the silo and windmill. Blowing smoke and ashes marked the grave of the barn.

At last he could see the house bobbing between Moxie's ears. The hole burned in the roof seemed to gape in surprise at the cloudy sky.

A figure burst out of the garage and waved his hat and kept on waving as Drew came nearer and saw that it was Dad.

Moxie sailed past him on the way to the stock tank, where he buried his nose in the muddy water. Billy Boy lapped beside him.

Drew dismounted stiffly and turned to face his father. Time to pay for all his mistakes, he thought.

Dad swept Drew into his arms and clasped him tightly, lifting him clear off the ground. "I've been tryin' for hours to get that danged car started to come looking for you," he said against Drew's neck.

Drew hugged him back. He could not be sure, but he thought he saw tears on his father's face as he slid to his feet. "Dad, I found Poke, but he wouldn't come home with me. He said he'll be home someday, though."

"I figured that's where you'd gone." Dad straightened but kept an arm about Drew's shoulder. "We thought you were lost, son. Come on in the house and tell us all about it."

Drew hesitated. "Sure, Dad. But first I got to look after Moxie and Billy Boy. They've been through a lot." He glanced up to see Mom standing in the screen door, tears glistening in her eyes. He opened the door, hopped up to the top step, and pecked her on the cheek.

She grabbed him and held him to her fiercely. "Thank God," she breathed. "You worried us half to death!"

Dad's gaze met Mom's. "Poke's decided to make his own way now." He grinned at Drew and wiped his eyes. "I'm just thankful we'll still have our Man of the Year for a little while longer."

Drew blinked rapidly. "Dad, Poke said you're going to stay? Are we, Dad? We'll have the sheep money and the wheat allotment, and we can sell Granddad's gold watch to buy groceries and feed for just enough stock to start over. Can't we stay?"

Dad nodded slowly. "But you understand nothing has really changed. We'll still be scrambling in the dust and scratching for our next meal and trying to hang on for a long time to come."

Thunder boomed overhead, then rolled across the prairie. Drew grinned. "Listen, Dad! We've got to get up there and nail some tin over that hole in the roof. It's going to rain!"

His mother relaxed her hold on Drew at last. "And I must clean the kitchen while it's a bit cooler and see if I can't find something special! You must be starved. With only the three of us . . ." She patted Drew's cheek and let the screen door slam behind her.

With his hands in his back pockets, Dad leaned back to study the clouds. "Maybe it's just teasing us, same as always." Even in the blowing dust Drew could see the hint of a smile on his father's face. "And maybe it ain't."